I0623284

Club El Diablo:

Damian

Holly S. Roberts

Club El Diablo: Damian

Holly S. Roberts

Copyright © 2018 Holly S. Roberts

Edited by Mechelle Kowalsky
Cover Art by Fantasia Frog Designs

All rights reserved. No portion of this book may be multiplied, stored in a retrieval system, transmitted in any form or by whatever means. Electronic, mechanical, photocopying, recording, or otherwise without express written permission of the writer. This eBook is licensed for your use only.

This is a work of fiction. ALL characters are derived from the author's imagination.

No person, brand, or corporation mentioned in this Book should be taken to have endorsed this Book nor should the events surrounding them be considered in any way factual.

Dedication

To all the freaks. Let's be freaks together.

Biography

Holly S. Roberts is the USA TODAY Best-Selling author of more than 30 books. She lives high in the Arizona Mountains with her husband and two spoiled dogs.

Chapter One

Lydia

The whip snaps with just enough force to bring a low cry from Angela's lips. When I use the four-foot Australian leather in a scene, it always draws a large crowd. The sound of breathing from those gathered surrounds me and I can feel the sexual excitement in the air. I stay in the zone, and so does my sweet sub. Angela is one of my favorites to work with—her surrender is beautiful.

Moisture beads along my hairline as my arm rises and I flick the whip again. Red welts, never breaking the skin, systematically appear down Angela's back. The people watching grow quieter as the scene continues. This is what members of the Mediterranean Club pay for. Though calling this place a club is going slightly overboard. MC is a dive. I've worked here for three years and done everything from tend bar to discipline subs. My current role of enacting scenes for the questionable crowd is my favorite. I blank out the whispered voices, the smell of sex, and too many bodies. Angela needs me. And I need Angela too.

The domination of this scene fulfills the place inside me that craves release. My thoughts calm with each strike. Angela's small gasp when I place a stinging stripe to the tender skin of her upper thigh sizzles through me. Here... I am master.

Fortunately, the club's owner appreciates the crowd I draw and lets me clean and maintain my own alcove. I also have a small office off the back where I soothe and comfort my patrons after I finish breaking down their submissive barriers. Yes, it's a dive but it's my space in this fucked up world.

I give Angela a brief respite so I can adjust the speed of the vibrator clenched within her tight pussy and turn her around so I have a clean canvas. The scent of her sweat and desire floats through me. Her moans grow louder with the absence of stimulation and I rotate my wrist, ready for the next round. *Snap.* I love the sound as it pops against flesh.

She can no longer hold back her screams and she finds release. The orgasm ripples through her body, carrying the crowd with her. Many of the watchers pull their subs aside for a small moment of relief before the next show begins. I have one more exhibition for the evening and then I can go home. I haven't used my personal toys on myself in more than a week, and I need a little private fantasy time.

I remove the vibrator from between Angela's legs and assist Raul in releasing the sobbing woman from her bindings. He carries her nude body into my small private domain and gently places her on a low, padded bench.

"I'll take it from here, Raul. Thank you."

"Yes, Mistress Lydia," he nods. We're best friends, but he follows protocol when I'm working. Angela rests on her side shuddering and trying to control her emotions. I walk over, run my hand gently through her hair, and help her sit up to take a sip of the orange juice I offer.

"Thank you, Mistress."

"You did wonderful tonight, Angela. I don't think I've ever seen you more beautiful and responsive." I kiss her cheek and take out a bottle of my personal blend of special oils to coat the red welts I left on her skin. I also want to make sure I haven't caused any lasting damage. There is no sign of blood or torn skin, but I like to assure myself the subs are okay before they leave my private room.

"Lay back, sweetheart, and I'll get you fixed up so you feel better."

"Yes, Mistress." Her gruff voice is subspace lazy, and I smile softly at the worn out picture she presents.

I help her to her stomach and began soothing the oil into the silky soft skin of her legs, back, and ass. "Tell me about your week." I keep my voice gentle. This is her time and her reward for giving me her trust. I listen attentively and make the proper sounds of encouragement when called for.

"He didn't call," she whispers with such hopelessness that it twists my heart. "I waited all week and now I know he won't be back. I loved him, but he won't accept me for who I am."

"When's the last time you saw your therapist, Angela?" I arranged for this particular therapist. Donna, a sub herself, understands the D/s dynamic and Angela needs someone who won't frown on her lifestyle.

"I saw her two weeks ago. She told me Aaron probably wasn't the guy for me, but I was still hoping he would give us a chance."

"Is that why you requested I use the whip tonight?" I usually don't give into requests. My subs trust that I know what's best for them. Something in Angela's eyes as she kneeled before me had me granting consent.

"Yes, Mistress, I needed to forget the rest of the world. Thank you."

My hands continue gliding gently over her firm buttocks and upper thighs. Angela's body is beautiful. Each curve a work of art. If I were gay, I would be in love with this messed up, beautiful woman. The men in her life are just plain stupid. Angela would give that special someone the world if they would look beyond her need for pain. "Turn over and let me attend your front."

I rub the oil into her breasts, upper thighs, and stomach. Toward the end of the scene, I'd struck her perfectly groomed pussy a few times because I knew it would take her over the top. Now, I make sure to massage the faint red lines to take away the sting.

Angela's breathing quickens but she knows my rules—no sex outside of a scene or you are no longer one of my treasured subs. I'm strict and never deviate from my rules. It's all in the not-so-fine print of the contract they sign before I begin working with them. Why I think my rules keep me from forming attachments I'm not sure. I have deep feelings for Angela. No, they aren't sexual and Angela isn't the only sub I care about. It's important to me that I define our connections and control them. My entire world at the club revolves around control.

"You're beautiful, Angela." I pluck her nipples with a little twist and she groans in response. I kiss her cheek and help her sit up. Grabbing a soft towel from a shelf below the bench, I wrap it around her and take a quick peek at the time. I have forty-five minutes until my next scene. Angela needs me more than I need my low-cal snack break. We sit on the couch and my sweet little sub asks permission to lay her head in my lap. My fingers run through her lush, blonde strands and I listen while she speaks more about her life.

It's times like this that everything becomes clear and I take solace from my poor fucked up life with human touch and caring. I sip on bottled water and give Angela a full bottle to make sure she stays hydrated. I hate post-scene sub drop, and having this bonding time helps us both avoid the aching loneliness of our lives for a little longer.

"Are you going home now or will you hang around for a while?" I ask. I know the Mediterranean Club is not the best place for Angela after a scene, but there's little I can do but ask Raul to keep his eyes on her. In my contract I gain the right to act as a service top. This limits my ability to boss Angela around even though I know she wouldn't mind. This is another way I keep my D/s relationships on an even keel. It's worked so far so and I have no plans to stop now. Because of my own personal sexual needs I stay away from permanent D/s relationships.

She gazes up at me with absolute trust. "I'm going home, but I'll make an appointment with you for next week if I may, Mistress."

"Yes, but I'll miss you until then." Angela moves slightly and the towel slips off her breasts. Her creamy soft skin practically begs for attention. No, it won't be from me. I lift Angela's head slightly and take her lips in a soft lingering kiss. The door to my private world opens and my gaze travels to the sound. One hand clenches suddenly in Angela's hair, though I soften my grip immediately and lower her back to my lap.

"This room is off limits. Please leave and close the door behind you." I expect the door to shut immediately but an unfamiliar man takes a full step into my domain. I can only stare. He's well over six feet tall, breathtakingly gorgeous, and ever so lickable. With two more aggressive strides he's completely inside my private sanctuary. It's more than obvious his hot body doesn't belong at the MC. He puts off a killer dominant vibe but that special place inside me hopes he's submissive. I instantly want to control every inch of him. Oh, but to punish first for disobeying me. My pussy grows wet.

I hold Angela still as her muscles tense and she tries to move her head from my lap.

"If you take another step, I'll have security throw you out of the club and have your membership revoked." It's the best I can come up with. What I really want is to replace the date with my vibrator later on and use the stud standing inside my door. I rarely orgasm at the club, but for this man I might bend my rules a little.

He offers a tight smile. "I'm afraid it's your boss who gave me permission to come in here." His smooth, powerful voice sends goose bumps across my skin, damn him. His dark dangerous eyes hold mine and the secret spark I hide from the world flares. To have his hands punishing me would be— I snap my thoughts from going there. What happens in my bedroom stays in my bedroom not in this sleazy club. His gaze travels to Angela, lying nearly naked in my lap, before zeroing in on me again. Angela's body trembles noticeably in my arms. I run my hand through her hair, though it's purely a nervous gesture, and crap, I'm never nervous. He's just so cocky, and an inkling of who is standing in my domain has entered my lust-filled brain. Anger slowly replaces thoughts of domination.

"Angela, my sweet, our time is up. Thank you for sharing your beautiful body and giving me your pleasure. Come in early next week and I'll buy you a drink. I'd like to try a new scene and I think it will push you just a bit more." Looking up into the intense eyes watching me, I lean forward and take Angela's mouth. This time I put a bit more carnal movement into my lips. As if on cue, she responds instantly. I know better and I didn't mean to tease her, but Mr. Dominance shook me up.

I pull away from the kiss and gather the towel around her shoulders. "Get dressed and when you're ready to leave the club Raul will escort you to your vehicle." I put command in my voice so she hopefully won't consider defying me. The parking lot has no security to speak of. "I'll see you next week."

I assist her past Mr. Umm He Smells Delicious. Glancing out the door, my eyes find Raul, who is cleaning my area for the next scene. I give him my "you will be punished" look for not warning me about my visitor, but then I nod toward Angela so he can take over. Raul and I are a team and he knows Angela requires close attention after a scene. I shut the door when the two walk away.

My eyes skim slowly up the large, yummy male body standing before me. He's wearing black loafers, black pants, and a long-sleeved white dress shirt unbuttoned halfway down his remarkable chest. His muscles bulge beneath the shirt, which makes the entire package sexier. They aren't the over the top muscles of a competing body builder but with a little oil, he could make a statement. His skin is darker than a suntan would provide and I guess he has Native American, Hispanic, or another darker-skinned race somewhere in his bloodline. He's gorgeous. I've heard the rumors about him through the BDSM grapevine but seeing Damian in person is different. For the first time in years, my pussy yearns for action from a man at the club.

I'm non-club exclusive when I fuck, and it takes a lot of work to bring me over the edge. I have a feeling this man could do it without touching me. His dominance rolls off him in waves of pleasure pheromones. He's trouble and it doesn't help that he knows how insanely sexy he is. I'm sure he just blinks those luscious dark eyes and women drool as an orgasm rocks their world. I hope the saliva in my mouth stays where it is and I get through this without making a complete fool of myself.

When my eyes finally lock on his, he quirks his mouth slightly and I notice dimples that only make him more arresting. I bet he hates those dimples. Somehow, I manage to control my breathing. I'm not the best Domme in the state for nothing. My cool gaze meets his—one master to another.

"Mr. Collins, you've taken me by surprise. I thought I was clear in my refusal of your offer." *Thought* had nothing to do with it. I made myself very fucking clear. Even so, I decide to play nice for the moment.

His chocolate eyes pierce mine. "I was told you only fuck men." He is obviously holding back a grin, but he purposely lets his dimples flash in a well-practiced expression that must drive women crazy. I'm not just any woman, though. I have control from the top of my head to the tips of my toes. I just need to convince my pussy to calm down, or dry up as the case might be.

My spine straightens as my resolve to resist his charm intensifies. "I don't discuss my sexual preferences with strangers," I scold him. Take that you sexy demon and smoke it in your penis pipe.

This time he smiles full out, his teeth pearly white and straight. His lips are so incredibly luscious I envy them. My knees weaken and my heart races. Years of hiding my own inadequacies make me stand tall in the face of Michelangelo's *David*. I am really in trouble, but I'll be damned if I allow him to see it.

His body stiffens and for the first time since he entered my domain, I see a flash of annoyance in his dark eyes. It's nice to know I can bend his impeccable control. His voice is as smooth as before. "I don't particularly care about your sexual preferences, but I paid a lot of money to find out what makes you tick and I wasn't expecting surprises." His voice changes and he allows a touch of irritation to enter it. "I can't say I'm thrilled to fly halfway across the country to handle what should have been a cut and dry deal you couldn't refuse. I'm not fond of the word 'no,' so here I am at this less-than-stellar establishment." He peers up at the rain-stained ceiling. It no longer leaks, but the evidence of the past makes it look as if the roof might cave in. His eyes zip back to mine. "Seeing it in person is far worse than the pictures my team provided. I'm at a complete loss about your reasons for refusing to work for me."

This is his Dom voice, and it's enough to snap me out of my lovesick fantasies of taking his hard cock in my mouth and making him moan. Years of practice help me control my emotions. Unfortunately, there's nothing I can do about the fire blazing in my eyes. My complexion turning from pale to red is the bane of light skin, freckles, and red hair that hangs in a single roped braid down my back. I have a Dom voice too and use it with every inflection required to make a sub shake in their invisible boots. "You've wasted your time for nothing," I snap. "There's absolutely no need for you to *slum* in my neck of the woods. My answer was final, is final. No!"

His expression remains intense and his eyes flash with enough fire to match mine. "Your boss feels differently," he tosses out.

"My boss can't afford to lose me." Johnny Ford knows I'm his bread and butter and I draw beginners and BDSM legends to his slimy-assed club. At five foot six and a hundred and forty pounds, I'm not small. It took years to turn my extra pounds into muscle. Those muscles can wield a whip to perfection. I have come to terms with my large framed body. Damn, Damian Collins makes me wish I were five two and built like Angela. Argh, the man is a devil as his name suggests. He needs to leave.

Damian's eyes relax and his lips quirk at the sides. He thinks he's won and I have no idea why. I'm afraid I'm about to learn, though. "Your boss has been well-compensated for your time and he's placed you at my disposal for the next thirty days."

Hot fury rushes through me and steam might actually pour from my ears, eyes, and nose. This Neanderthal is not buying me. No fucking way. "I am not for sale, Mr. Collins." Regardless of my flushed skin, my tone is glacial. "To you or by my ex-boss. Emphasis on ex." I storm across the room and, using the key I keep on top of the cabinet, I open my locker and retrieve my large personal bag. It holds my street clothes along with sub toys, but there is no way I'm changing here. If a cop stops me on my way home, he gets an eyeful and maybe I'll get out of a ticket. I don't see myself driving slowly and obeying the speed limit and I *will* pay the damn ticket if it comes to that.

Refusing to look at Mr. Dick on a Stick, I make sure I have everything that belongs to me. I won't be back and the sick feeling in my stomach along with my watery eyes only pisses me off more. I refuse to let it sway me and only have one goal before I leave. I will kick Johnny Ford in the balls like I should have done too many times to count.

I turn to the door but the cream-dream fantasy man in my office blocks the path, his back rests against the scarred wood with his arms crossed in such a... a dominant manner. "I'm taking you to dinner to discuss my proposal."

The arrogant ass. My eyes travel to the corner camera. It might be my private room but for safety reasons the cameras are essential. The problem is Johnny knew how I would react, and I can only guess the amount of money it took for him to give me up for a month. Damn him, he won't be sending a bouncer to get me out of my current predicament.

I have no choice and even with years of self-defense, I have little chance of removing my problem physically. His broad shoulders brush both sides of the doorframe. God, I love a large chest and a man who makes me feel small. Controlling my inner slut, I snap out of lust and into disgust. My only means of escape will happen after I leave this office.

I meet Mr. Dreamsicle's eyes. "Well, the answer to your proposal will still be no, but I would never refuse a free dinner." I can't hide all my irritation, but my voice drops a sexy notch. I'm a good actress.

His grin flashes again. He steps back and opens the door so I precede him. I do my best to not breathe as I scrape past him. Oh God, his spell. *No, I do not like man smell and ham. I do not like them Lydia I am.* The litany in my head actually calms me somewhat and I'm throwing these panties away as soon as I'm home. My pussy is betraying me and the panties will take the blame.

Chapter Two

Damian

Why am I here? I've asked myself this question since my plane landed in California. This woman is driving me insane. I wake up almost nightly from dreams where my fingers are caught in her incredible hair, her head tipped back, and my lips a whisper from hers. My hard-on pulses to some unknown beat that only this woman orchestrates.

I'm Damian Collins. I have everything—more money than I could spend in several lifetimes, friends who support me, and women to dominate and fulfil my every fantasy. Actually, it's a dangerous combination. The amount of personal wealth I've amassed means the world is my playground and I can buy anything, and I mean anything. I have a friend who fights against human sex trafficking because of men in my situation who don't hold themselves to higher principles.

The flurries of Mistress Lydia entered my private world and I've been on a mission since. I admit I was only intrigued at first. Then, I wanted her working for me. Now, for the damnedest reason, I just want her. It makes no sense and this type of obsession is dangerous.

Hell.

Seeing her kiss the sub sent a wave of jealousy trough me. I'm never fucking jealous. I have over a twenty photos of Lydia, collected by my private investigator, while she's in the club and when she's away from it. I've stared at them for hours trying to figure out what it is about her that makes me want her so much. Meeting her in person only proves that every Goddess rumor is true. Her reputation as a beautiful dominant who can bring almost anyone to their knees is also true and I resent the fact that I want to drop to mine. This isn't me. I put the gear shift in control freak and I dominate, period.

Oh, I've played the other card because a true dominant needs to understand what it means to give up control. I wasn't very good at it then and I wouldn't be now. Even for her. So why the hell do I want her?

Female dominants have it hard enough. I know this and have seen it with my own eyes. They aren't taken seriously in so many circles. This woman breathes exactly who and what she is. So, again, why the fuck is my cock hard and my brain begging for a chance to slip my dick in between her hot lips?

My thoughts return to the sub who left. I'm a man. Two women kissing is fucking sexy or at least usually it is. I wanted to tear that little subby away, rest my head in Lydia's lap, and grind her lips down against mine. The second kiss Lydia gave the sub didn't matter. That was for show. And why did Lydia feel the need to show me anything?

I read the contempt in her eyes. I also see something else. I would be stupid to consider it desire. So what the hell is it? I can't believe she gave in this easily. I inhale deeply as she walks by. My cock chimes in with a sudden jolt at her scent. Sweat and desire are mixed with a unique fragrance that is hard to place. They say the sense of smell is the last to go. I will never forget this combination and will fucking jack off to the memory as soon as I have the chance.

"After you, Lydia," I say when she hesitates to enter the club proper. I want to see her ass. I want to imagine driving my cock deep and listening to her moan. I want to think the scent of desire she carries is for me. I just plain fucking want this woman.

Chapter Three

Lydia

I keep my office brighter than the low-to-no light in the main part of the club. It takes a moment for my eyes to adjust after I walk in. Unfortunately, this isn't a good thing. I often think blindness would be better than looking at these crappy surroundings. The darkness does nothing to hide the sleazy atmosphere.

I figure Johnny shopped at the BDSM equivalent of a garage sale or he gathered donations off curbsides where people hoped someone could benefit from their castoffs. Slimy surroundings go hand in hand with my slimy ex-boss. No more, I'm finished.

I'm finished with putting up with his shit and finished wondering why I stay. He basically sold me. I don't care if we have a working relationship—nothing I've done would give him the audacity to think he could sell my time. But he did, the bastard.

Damian doesn't touch me as I walk past, but he uses his large frame to crowd my body on purpose. The man has nerve and entirely too much alpha sex appeal. I cast an angry glare at a group of subs sitting on a garish couch with their mouths hanging open while they watch the man behind me. Too bad I won't be around to give a little discipline. I notice one of my regulars, Molly, sitting with them. Like a good sub, she keeps her eyes down. She's pretty and overweight by about fifty pounds. I'm sure she wouldn't make it past the door of Mr. Edible's exclusive, ultra-rich, private club. If I still weighed over two hundred pounds, I wouldn't be in this stupid predicament. Mr. Crocodile Teeth would want nothing to do with me. Maybe I'll eat a cherry tart tonight. Hell, maybe I'll eat two.

I take a deep breath and as much as I hate to admit it, I am pissed at being forced to leave this smelly, seedy place that is my second home. It's where I can be myself and not worry that I'm too brash for a woman or even too smart. The club might be the sleazy equivalent of a porn arcade but it holds all the memories of finding my niche in this world.

Out of the corner of my eye, I catch sight of Johnny. I turn toward him, but a strong hand wraps around my forearm. Electricity pulses across my skin. Damian's hand is hot and dry on my sweaty flesh. He not so gently leads me away from the hairy balls that need my knee. "I'd like a word with my boss," I say while trying to unobtrusively pull away. The subs are watching and the fact only pisses me off more.

"No." His fingers tighten. "And if you cause a scene I'll pick you up and carry you over my shoulder. Your choice." His words leave no way to misinterpret the meaning. He's using his Dom voice too.

I come to a sudden stop and his grasp on my arm actually hurts. I look up into the dark eyes that hold a promise—he would enjoy my humiliation. No one tops me outside of my bedroom. This Neanderthal Romeo can't know that. He has no idea what my sexual peculiarities are. He only knows I'm dominant. Why does he think he can control me? I'm completely fed up and if Johnny is getting rid of me and won't send backup to help, I need to handle this myself.

Using my body, I step into Mr. Deluxe Dimples, and in perfect textbook Self Defense 101, I grab his arm, tip my shoulder, and bend at the waist. Taking another step in, I twist and lean to the side sending Mr. Tall, Dark, and Airborne flying. The entire move takes less than two seconds. Before he makes a solid thump against the cheap carpet, I'm heading out the front door just daring the bouncers to stop me.

I clear the entrance, debating if now is a good time to run. I'm not concerned about what's ahead of me—I'm terrified by what I left behind. I cast a quick look over my shoulder.

"Are you Ms. Simmons?"

Shit. I can't help my startled squeal. Two hundred and fifty pounds of double trouble stands before me leaning against a black limousine. I am so fucking screwed. At that moment, Mr. Maniac comes through the door. His dimples are no longer on display. I'm guessing he didn't enjoy looking like a fool in front of a bunch of subs.

His voice is deadly. "If she gets away, you're fired."

There isn't time to run because ham hocks wrap tightly around my arms and lift me off the ground.

"Toss her in the back seat," Mr. Airborne snaps.

"You son of a bitch, this is kidnapping," I yell. It's not like anyone will notice, but I'm too upset to think past what's happening. I'm scared and it pisses me off more if that's even possible. I kick my foot back and Mr. Muscleman Number Two lets out a grunt.

The car door opens and a not-so-gentle hand pushes me between my shoulder blades. I'm wearing knee-high black boots and a short black leather mini skirt with a red thong beneath. My knees hit the side of the limo and I fall forward with my ass in the air. A solid hand slaps down across my displayed cheeks and I scramble inside. I crawl to the far corner and sit on the same aforementioned body part.

I am beyond furious and like many women would be, even a dominant one, I'm at the point of tears. Things are not pretty when I cry. Biting my tongue finally causes enough pain to hold back the emotion. I think about screaming at the top of my lungs to release the panic eating me alive but Mr. Moron and his muscle-bound sidekick would only get pleasure out of my loss of control.

The front door of the car slams and we immediately roll forward, picking up speed as we turn out of the parking lot. I catch a quick glimpse of Raul rushing out the door and watching the tail end of my kidnapping. I turn my head toward my nemesis. If this is his idea of a job interview, he's insane.

I have repeatedly turned down the offers to work at Club El Diablo even though it's the most exclusive private sex club in the country. Raul thinks I'm a fool but at the MC, I run things my way. I choose my subs based on my needs and theirs. I also understand that poor self-esteem brings many men and women into this lifestyle. I meet the desires of the needy and I put up with fast-fingered Johnny because the MC fills an empty hole inside of me.

I want nothing to do with slapping my whip against the asses of the rich and lazy who think their shit doesn't stink. I sit in my corner of the limo fuming for about sixty seconds.

"Where are you taking me?" I finally demand grudgingly.

He doesn't immediately answer. A typical Dom response—build the tension and let the little sub know who's in charge. I grit my teeth and breathe deeply through my nose to control myself.

I can't see his dark eyes in the shadowed back seat, but his tone when he speaks sends shivers down my spine. "My plan was to take you to dinner, but quite truthfully I'm now thinking my private suite would be the best place to put you across my knee and redden the rest of your sweet ass."

I inhale sharply, unable to keep the sound from escaping. Damn, my panties will start leaking soon. They're barely a scrap of material as it is. I'll leave a huge wet spot on the car seat and Mr. Beckoning Balls will see exactly what he does to me.

I sit up straight and clench my fists so hard I know my fingernails will leave marks on my palms. "You seem to have me mistaken for one of your subs. If you think you can beat me into accepting your job offer, you'll be disappointed."

Chapter Four

Damian

If any woman ever needed a spanking, it's this one. When she performed her little move on me, I wasn't expecting it and hit the ground before I could come up with a countermove. Yeah, I'm angry and that's never good.

This is a lifestyle of choice. I've never before laid a hand on a woman who didn't want it. They might be afraid because a punishment spanking is no cake walk, but they voluntarily suffer the consequences for their actions. Punishing this woman, a dominant, goes against everything I believe in. She's driven me completely, certifiably insane, because I'm contemplating a fitting punishment.

I have no idea what to do now. A dominant doesn't make threats he's unwilling to see through. I need to calm the fuck down. I've never been into choking but the thought of putting my hands around her throat is as pleasant as striking the palm of my hand across her ass.

I wanted to see that very ass walk in front of me. I got more than I bargained for when Carl tossed her into the car. God, her ass cheeks begged for exactly what I gave them and that one slap is not nearly enough. Plain and simple, she brings out the worst in me. I should be shoving her out the door and not contemplating locking her in a room and keeping her against her will. Christ, fuck, what am I thinking?

My friend Monroe would kick my ass. He's the one who fights against sex trafficking. There's no excuse for my behavior and I need to take control back. I give Lydia my disappointed Dom face. "Oh? I have no intention of beating you in order to get you to accept my offer. I plan to spank your delectable ass to make myself feel better." Take that, you sexy as sin pain in my ass.

I can't quite see her eyes but I can feel their heat. With all that red hair, her fiery temper just adds to the turn on. "If you hit me again, I'll file charges," she challenges.

My laughter fills the car. Wealth can buy many things, including enough legal mumbo jumbo to keep the charges tied up in the court process for years. She doesn't worry me. "I assure you, my team of attorneys will handle any legal problems you throw my way."

"Why me?" she whispers. For the first time, I hear defeat in her tone. I don't like it and the faint echo of her words finally gets through to me. I'm being a complete out of control ass. If anything can be salvaged from this fiasco, I need to try.

Holly S. Roberts

Chapter Five

Lydia

I don't trust this man as far as I can throw him, so why is his voice sizzling across my skin like a Fourth of July sparkler?

"Your fame precedes you, and I'm tired of hearing about the red-headed Domme who attracts my rich patrons. They fly over here at least once a month just to watch you work. They pay your boss big bucks for a chance to have you top them, but it seems you are rather discerning in your choice of subs. I only know of one person who managed to get past your selection process. It's been the talk of my club for months." His Dom voice has turned low and sexy. I'm sure it's easy for him to turn it on and off given that he's completely in charge.

What I would give to tie him up and make him groan. I'd put the largest plug I could find up his ass and lock his cock in the smallest cage available. Hell, I'd add ginger oil to the plug and enjoy every minute he begs for mercy.

I'm lying to myself. If there were ever a man to top me, Damian's the one. In the privacy of my bedroom, it's what I crave—a Dom who controls me, brings me to my knees, and makes me beg. I'm a disgrace to Dommes everywhere. I'm not a switch, which makes my fantasies nearly impossible to obtain. The men I find to relieve the submission itch are never enough. It starts in bed and ends there. Well, not necessarily bed, but the second the scene is over, so is my submission.

Inhaling slowly to gain control of myself, I decide to give my abductor a small amount of truth. "I know the Mediterranean is a rat hole, but I'm not into perfect people. I enjoy flaws. Your mega million-dollar followers spend enough money keeping their bodies beautiful to feed a small country. My answer is no and will always be no."

He's silent for a few minutes and I'm fascinated that he's considering what I'm saying. "Hmm, you may have a point," he says at last. "They're beautiful, but I believe most of them are mentally fucked up. Mommy and Daddy didn't give them enough attention, rich Uncle Bruce got too touchy feely when they were young, or better yet, the dog was the only one willing to put out when they were juveniles."

I can't believe he said that. "You're disgusting."

His voice goes from sexy to stern. "And you're prejudice. I've seen your earlier pictures before your generous curves became muscled stealth. You put as much stock into your body as my millionaire club members do. I didn't find any evidence of plastic surgery in your file but borderline anorexia and maybe even bulimia are a given."

It's killing me that I can't see his face but at the same time, he can't see mine. My fingers tremble as I bring them to my mouth. It hurt—his words, his guess, and his obvious satisfaction in my humiliation. My hand goes to the door handle. I am getting out even if I need to jump. As my luck would have it, the door won't budge.

A touch of anger enters his voice. "Does the truth hurt?" He's angry, but there's something else too. I would give anything to know his story. "All of us are fucked up in this crazy world. You don't need to be into the BDSM scene to be crazy and we both know it. I think you will be pleasantly surprised by the diverse nature of my... followers, as you call them. I want you working at Club El Diablo. I'm willing to negotiate terms. I'll give you a one-month trial period, a deluxe suite at my hotel, and allow Raul to accompany you, though he will officially work for me. You'll work three nights a week but no tending bar, helping with accounting, or cleaning your own area. I'll triple your pay plus pay the rent on your apartment so you have a place to come back to... if you come back."

Here we go again with his demands. He'll never understand. Part of my control is that I work at a place like the Mediterranean. Lost souls who don't judge me or if they do, they don't find me lacking. I won't fit in Damian's hobknob crowd. I'm still the fat girl with a huge chip on her lonely shoulder.

"If you remain stubborn and continue to say no, I offer a wager."

Shit. He's done his homework. This is my worst flaw; I live for a bet. It's my vice. Once a month I take my hidden savings and wager one hundred dollars on the ponies at the racetrack. I bring all my money so I can prove to myself that I don't have a problem. When the hundred is gone, I always walk away. It's my test.

Before he died, my father was a jockey. He never made the big time but he raised me at the track. He was five two and weighed a hundred pounds soaking wet. My mother was large like me but that's what turned him on. She died when I was a baby. My dad loved nothing more than telling me stories of the first time he saw her. As I grew older, his betting problem became a major factor in our life. Betting losses turned to drinking more alcohol. I loved him, but I never want to be weak like that.

I shake myself mentally and snap out of my walk down memory lane. I can't help myself because really, I am a betting girl. "Terms?" I ask even though I know I'm crazy.

His laugh vibrates across every nerve in my body. It's almost sexier than he is. "If you accept the challenge, I'll hold off on the spanking you deserve and drive you back to your car after dinner."

"Terms?" I demand in my ultimate bitch Domme voice.

Now he gives a heavy sigh. "You have twenty-four hours to hide and then I have twenty-four to find you, though I doubt I'll need it. If I win, and I will, you'll work for me for the desired thirty days. If you win, I'll pay you fifty thousand dollars and walk away."

Fuck, he must know I want my own club and he knows I need the money. Double fuck. "You have a deal, but I have one condition about dinner."

"That's okay. Carl take us to Beasty Burgers. My lady wants her usual."

I'm in so much fucking trouble.

Chapter Six

Damian

It took a naughty sub to discover what all the whispers in my club were about. She didn't want to tell me about the Domme in California who was attracting my expensive clientele.

"What's her name?" I asked after she finally surrendered.

The tears sliding down her face were caused by me and the cane I had just used on the backs of her thighs. "I don't know her real name. They call her the fiery Domme," she answered with trembling lips.

I loosened my grip on her hair and rubbed my thumb across those very same lips. "Why didn't you think you could tell me about her?" This is the question that's really bothered me. I keep my finger on the pulse of the BDSM community at all times. I'd known for weeks that something or someone was causing a stir. It wasn't an open whisper. It seems the subs have been playing on the side and didn't want the big bad Doms to know. There are no rules against this but it's odd. Once a sub makes a connection with a Dom, they usually ask for permission to play with someone else. I can't imagine a Dom denying them. It's against the Dom code unless they're in an exclusive relationship and even then, they would be released, not forbidden from going. What I really found strange was that both male and female subs seemed to be in thrall with the fiery Domme. I needed more answers than the sub could provide.

I unsnapped the naughty sub from her restraints and sent her on her way.

"But, Master—"

I cut her off. "You will not seek pleasure for seven days. The next time I ask you a question you will answer immediately." More tears slid down her cheeks. I love sub tears but licking them off would only give her pleasure and that's the last thing she deserved. I turned and walked away without giving her aftercare. Yeah, bad Dom move but I'm pissed off and she'll forgive me, eventually.

I have a private investigator on retainer. In my business it's important to keep a watch on my clientele. If they cross certain lines allowed by their bottomless bank accounts, I make sure they face the consequences. Finding Tilton was thanks to my relationship with Monroe. The man has connections all over the world. Exactly what Monroe does besides rescuing women and his art is beyond me. What I do know is that he's the deadliest SOB of my acquaintance. He's also the most talented. Monroe is a world-renowned Shibari artist.

I went to my office and made the call, giving Tilton as much information as I had. The three days I waited for his return call were strangely painful.

"I take it you've heard the rumors about a Domme stealing our thunder," Kyle, one of the club's more sadistic Doms, asked me on day two.

"It took a little work but yeah, I heard about her."

"I find it interesting. You know I don't form attachments with subs and rarely play with the same one twice?"

"I'm perfectly aware of your proclivities," I offer and try to keep the sadness out of my smile. Kyle has a dark secret that not many people know about, and, here at the club, I'm probably the only one.

He nods and I see a flash of sorrow in his eyes, which he quickly covers. "I had an appointment set up with Carla a few days ago. She never called to cancel, she just didn't show."

Carla is trouble. She leaches onto Doms, becomes territorial, and is always a pain in the ass. It surprised me that Kyle would be interested in her at all and I knew for a fact that the woman had more hard limits than Fort Knox. Not Kyle's hard core style at all.

"A weak moment, you ass," he answered my unspoken condemnation that must have shown on my face. "She bugged the front office for months about being put on my list. I turned her down each time and she still kept trying. I finally set her down and explained exactly what I would do and her hard limits be damned."

I raised my eyebrows because this is against the rules and Kyle knows it.

He ignored my heavy gaze. "She marched into the office and changed her hard limits and I still made her wait another month before I agreed. Does that sound like the type of scene a sub fails to show up for?"

Kyle scares the fuck out of most of the subs here. He doesn't play often because of the secret he keeps. He's great to have around and he helps endlessly with problems that arise. He'll be around for weeks at a time and then disappear for just as long. I respect him and I hope that someday he'll find the peace he deserves. "I take it she blew you off and flew to California." I actually wanted to laugh. I'm glad this mysterious Domme wreaked havoc with someone besides me.

He looked at me with an all-knowing Dom gaze. "What the fuck do you plan to do about it?" he asked with a smirk.

"Hire her, of course."

He laughed and continued laughing as he left my office.

The next day I received a small packet of information that included a few pictures. Unsurprisingly, her driver's license photo didn't do her justice. A sexy image of her walking into the Mediterranean Club piqued my interest, though.

Red hair—the fiery Domme. I think it was the hair that first did me in. It became the center of my fantasies. Handfuls of that hair tangled in my fingers as my cock slid down her throat. I had to know more and learn about every facet of her life. Tilton followed my directives to dig deep and with each batch of information, I became more enthralled. With every photo my cock grew harder. I continued playing with subs but the deep-seated enjoyment was missing. There was no helping it. The fiery Domme had to work for me.

Her answer was no.

It didn't matter what I offered. I knew she lived close to the poverty level. Hell, I knew her boss was a weasel. Her defiance made no sense and neither do my wet dreams. I'm not a teenage boy who can't control himself. At least not until it came to her. Even my mother knew something was up.

"Is it a woman?" she asked me around the third or fourth "no" from Lydia.

"No," I answered. "Just restless." Was I lying? I wasn't sure. Lydia Simmons was the most exasperating woman on earth. She's also entirely out of reach for my sexual needs. I told myself that if she were working in my club, the fascination would fade.

My mother gave me a stern look and let it go.

It took two more months for me to get on a plane. Now I'm taking Lydia to her favorite fast food grease pit because after studying her history, I know when she's upset, she comes here to realign whatever it is that makes her tick. Watching her enjoy the hamburger catches me by surprise. I know all about her eating disorder and using the knowledge earlier to hurt her was a low blow. I'm better than that. This messed up woman deserves better than me. She deserves a sub who will worship her and give her loyalty. So why the hell am I playing this game?

Chapter Seven

Lydia

They drop me off at my car with a full stomach. Damian, as he insists I call him, stands in the parking lot watching me drive away. I head straight home. Samson needs his walk and I need to call Raul.

I know exactly where I'm going and I know no dossier, no matter how detailed, will have the information. Mr. Brutish Bristles can eat my wet panties and choke on them. I open the door of my apartment and one hundred and fifty pounds of lovable Rottweiler bounces around like a toy poodle. Samson and Raul are my best friends. Both give me so much more than I can ever give them in return. Sam follows me to my bedroom, where I change into sweats and running shoes.

My apartment is small, not in the best area, and the thin walls make it almost unbearable. The couple next door rocks their bed at all hours and I lay awake wondering what life would be like if I had a man in my life on a regular basis. My bedroom is little more than a closet with a double bed that practically touches both side walls.

I stand at the foot of the bed, unzip my boots, remove my leather corset and skirt, and then peel off the wet, red, dental floss that passed for panties. The evidence of my betrayal is in the damp lace, and I toss it on top of the corset. Walking over to the mirror is a mistake because when I look over my shoulder at my ass, a diminishing pink handprint is still visible. I run my fingers over the mark, which has no raised welts, damn him.

I pull on my favorite sweats, hiding the evidence of Mr. Control Freak's punishment. "Come on, monster, I have a Beasty Burger to work off and you need to do your business."

We run five miles through the disreputable neighborhood, taking breaks for Sam's personal needs. I love running in the dark and no one messes with me due to my four-legged bodyguard. The strain to my muscles feels wonderful. When I stop running and begin my mile cool down, I use my cell to call Raul. His mother has a dilapidated cabin she left him when she died. It's over two hundred miles away and we have only gone there once to clean and make sure everything was locked up tight. There is no electricity, no running water, and no way Mr. Delectable Dessert can discover my location.

By the time I return to my apartment, Raul is waiting in front with the cabin key. I jog up to his car and he whistles. "That man is edible. The rumors do him no justice," Raul says, obviously in lust again. Raul is gay and I'm unsurprised Mr. Hot Pants had this effect on him.

"I have no idea which way he swings, so you might have a chance," I tell him even though my heart clenches at the thought Damian Collins could be gay.

"Nope, I would have known if he swings my way. Gaydar and all that," he says with a wink. "You better watch yourself because your voice actually goes dreamy when you *don't* say his name."

"Bullshit," I lie. What Raul said terrifies me. There is no way I can allow Damian to see my inner weakness.

"Oh, sweetie, you're blushing," he says with a half-smile. Raul knows my secret. Hell, he sets me up on sex dates when I become super bitchy and dominance or my personal array of vibrators isn't doing it for me. I have to play this cool, though. The last thing I need is Raul thinking he can set me up with Mr. Chaotic Cock himself. "Stop, or I'll sick Sam on you and you'll drown in slobber," I respond as a way to change the subject. "I'm taking a quick shower, packing a bag, and then I'm gone for forty-eight hours. Fifty thousand dollars will get us started, Raul. Our club will be small but with our savings and the fifty grand, we can do it."

Raul's smile is something to behold. He's gorgeous and if it's the last thing I do, I'll find him the perfect Dom. "I know baby girl. Good luck," he says with a brief kiss on my cheek after I lean in and give him one.

One hour later, I'm on my way. Normally I would be sleeping now, so I crank the Rolling Stones up high and sing along. I won't win any singing competitions but I know every word to every Stones song ever recorded. When it comes to music, I'm a seventies wannabe. George Thorogood's "Bad To The Bone" plays next and I manage to stay awake. As the drive continues, Samson whines in the back whenever I hit a high note. I continually look in the rearview mirror, making sure no one follows.

Finally, my headlights lead the way through trees, avoiding the thick brush trying to take over the narrow dirt road. It hasn't rained in several weeks and my old Subaru Outback has no difficulty getting through the deep, dry ruts. After the next bump, my lights shine on a small cabin in the distance. Samson will enjoy this. I have two gallons of water, dog food, some canned food for me, and a six-pack of Sterno fuel. My biggest problem will be using the outhouse for the call of nature. Yuk. Good thing I can survive anything for two days.

Samson jumps out of the car as soon as the door opens. He immediately starts sniffing out his territory while I grab my small overnight bag and head to the cabin door. I leave the headlights on so I can see while unlocking the door. The car lights shine into the bare living room. Thank God I brought a book and candles to get me through the isolation. I carry my bag to the single bedroom that at least has a bed. The car light barely makes it around the curve of the door, but I can see enough to place my bag on the foot of the bed.

I turn and let out a blood-curdling scream as large arms shut the bedroom door and grab me in a steel grip, placing a hand over my mouth.

Samson hits the solid door with growls and barking.

A seductive voice whispers warmly in my ear. "I've won, Mistress Lydia. Your flight leaves tomorrow evening. Get some sleep and then get that delectable ass of yours home. Pack a few personal items. I'll provide everything else. The plane tickets are waiting on your kitchen counter. Samson and Raul are both provided for and will be going with you." His hand slowly slides from my mouth and travels down my neck, causing all kinds of trouble with my already overtaxed heartrate.

"You cheated," I say between gasps for air. I do everything I can to ignore the electrical charge of his touch and the smell of his sexy cologne. I usually hate any type of processed smelly shit, but he takes pheromone experimentation to a new level. My skin continues to sizzle where his fingers trail.

"You lost, so take it like a Dom." The laughter in his voice makes me grit my teeth. "Carl will pick you up at the airport in Houston. I'll let you walk me out so your dog doesn't bite my legs off."

I hear what sounds like helicopter blades in the distance. I am so completely fucked.

Chapter Eight

Damian

Anyone who knows me knows I play dirty when I want something, but bribing her friend was low even for me. She left me no choice, though. I had to get her to Club El Diablo and end this obsession.

I make phone calls through the radio during the long, noisy ride home. Club El Diablo is a very small part of my empire. The El Diablo Hotel, where the club is located, is another. I work hard for what I have and I play harder. I'm in a dire mood when I arrive back at the hotel. I need relief from my perpetual state of blue balls Miss Simmons kept me in. I go straight to the penthouse and change into comfortable jeans and black boots. I have a private elevator, so I leave off my shirt. This is not my usual attire for the club, though there isn't really a dress code for Doms or Dommes. The clothes I have on say a sub is about to get her ass beat before I drive my dick into it as far as it will go.

I take the elevator to my club office, pick up my play bag, and go in search of the poor little subby who will fulfil my desires this evening. Even with their downcast eyes, I see them give me side-sweeping gazes. I walk to the carousel and watch it twirl by with hopeful subs looking out hoping to catch the eye of an available Dom.

The club is known as a place to safely play and experience the kinky lifestyle that's in vogue right now. The main play areas and private rooms take up half a floor of the hotel. Then there's a front office where people are processed. This includes paperwork for medical and other things that keep everything safe. You want to play in my club, you'll obey my rules. From visiting dignitaries from foreign countries to rock and roll bands, we have something kinky for almost everyone who can pay the price and pass our background check.

I breathe in the smell of sex that permeates the air and the cries of submissives. A woman with red hair goes by and I almost beckon her over. I stop myself. No red hair. A brunette catches my attention and I give her the nod when she goes by a third time and peeks at me while the brightly painted horse she's on glides up and down.

She gracefully steps off the carousel and drops to her knees in front of me. I don't know her name even though I've seen her around. She's on the plump side, exactly as I prefer. I enjoy a nice ass wiggle when I slap my hand or a paddle on it. Miss Simmons' ass is a little tighter than I care for, so why is it her ass I'm thinking about right now?

I cup my hand on the back of the sub's neck after moving her hair aside. I pull slightly upward so she stands. "What's your name?"

"Bunny, Master," she says in a soft voice.

I know it's not her real name, but that's acceptable here. I'm also not her Master. That's one thing about Club El Diablo that differentiates itself from other sex clubs and their protocols—this is the devil's playground and the club feeds most desires. If she wants to call me Master, I won't stop her.

I slide my fingers into the hair at her neck and tip her head back. "I'm in the mood to play rough. Ass play, heavy implements, and orgasm denial. Just to be clear, yours not mine. If you're interested, go to the front office and grab your limit sheet so I can read it. I'll meet you in the barbarian room."

Her eyes shine. "Yes, Master, I want to play.

I nod and send her off for the paperwork. Usually I would examine her file first but tonight I want someone fresh and new. I plan to push each and every limit this woman has. She may never play with me again, but that's okay. There are plenty of other subs waiting in line behind her.

I stride to the barbarian room, acknowledging other Doms and one Domme on my way. They thankfully don't stop me to talk. Room monitors are in place and hopefully no one breaks the rules bad enough for me to be called. I'm not in the mood to deal with a rich dick or pussy tonight.

A minute later, Bunny enters the room with the requested paperwork. "Kneel," I tell her after she hands it to me. "We'll be using quite a few of the toys in here, so look around and be sure you don't want to leave before we get started."

Her hazel eyes are large as she glances around the room. "No, Master, I'm good," she says. I smell her anticipation and that tiny scent of fear I crave.

I flip through the paperwork. She's not into wet play, which doesn't bother me in the least because piss and blood don't turn me on. To each their own. This room has a drain and is the backup wet room for the members who aren't squeamish about such play. The floors are cement and I'm well aware Bunny's knees are cold and aching by now. I place the papers on the table. "Go to the spanking bench, bend over, and separate those ass cheeks for me."

She rises quickly and walks seductively to the bench. My cock doesn't so much as twitch. I remove a butt plug from its plastic wrapping. Using my teeth, I rip the protection off and grab a tube of lube. "I hope you don't mind the size," I say with a laugh. She turns and looks at the plug in my hands as I walk closer.

"Nn... no, Master."

Oh, that quiver. It's one of the small things a Dom lives for. I walk behind her and she spreads her cheeks like the good little subby she is. I apply a generous amount of lube and work the plug in and out until it seats in her ass properly. She whines the slightest bit but stops when I slap her ass. We've only just begun to play and this is nothing.

An hour later, she's begging for release that I hadn't planned to give her and my cock is as flat as a nail-ridden tire. Bunny has nice welts down her backside and I've been administering wicked nipple clamps off and on since we started playing.

What the fuck is wrong with me? I look at Bunny and her brown hair changes to red making my cock twitch. I blink the fantasy away. This is unfair to Bunny. I leave the plug in and grab a vibrator.

"You've been a good girl. Come for me."

With a high-pitched squeal and enough shaking to make me think she's having a seizure, she goes off. When her orgasm slows, I remove the plug, followed by the vibrator and help her stand. I assist her to the couch, leave her for a minute, and grab some juice from the fridge. I walk back to her after turning the lights down and grabbing a soft towel off the shelf above the table. I walk back over and pull Bunny into my arms, holding her while she comes down.

"Master?" she asks.

"Yes, Bunny?"

"I would like to please you. I'll do whatever you ask."

I smooth her hair back from her face, wishing her hazel eyes were the burning green of Lydia's. Wanting to please is typical of subs, especially after an intense scene. That's why I followed the rules and read her paperwork before we began. "Shh, you pleased me. You did everything I requested." I cover her lips with my finger when she tries to respond.

If I close my eyes and allow my fantasy to take over, I can dream that the fiery Domme is the woman in my arms.

Chapter Nine

Lydia

I'm currently standing in my tiny kitchen glaring daggers at my ex-best friend. "You gave me up," I spit out with a snarl. I'm so angry and Raul is lucky I'm still speaking to him. Well not speaking exactly, I've been shouting for a good ten minutes.

Raul is usually timid and his sudden backbone does not help his case. "If you stop yelling long enough to listen, I'll explain."

"There is no explanation," I hiss. "You knew I had no desire to leave the MC. You knew I'd refused Mr. Cheating Skunk's offer several times and you knew we needed the fifty thousand dollars."

Raul's hand comes out of his pocket and he shows me a white slip of paper. My eyes briefly pass over the deposit slip and I freeze before launching into my next tirade. I glance at the total again. Two hundred and eighty-six thousand dollars is clearly printed on the slip. I stare dumbfounded at Raul.

"Damian offered me two hundred and fifty grand to give up your location and now we have over two hundred and eighty grand in the bank when it's added to what we already saved. He might have found you anyway, so I took it. He told me he would take the money back if I alerted you. We now have enough to start our club with a little to put aside as a nest egg. What would you have done?"

I have no words as the total draws my attention again. The idiot spent a quarter million dollars to find my location. I almost hyperventilate as I stand there in stunned disbelief.

Raul's strong arms circle me and he pulls me into his hard male chest. He's like a brother and his embrace is comforting considering the rug has been pulled from beneath my feet. How can I fault him for taking the money? Hell, I would have taken the money. Our dream is currently sitting in the bank.

My eyes tear. "You know I didn't mean everything I just said?" I mumble into his shirt.

He smiles. "Oh, but I liked the gay fag stag comment. I might use it sometime."

"You bastard." My arms tighten and Sam whines. He hates when he isn't getting his share of attention. I sniff and pull back. "It's time to go. I sincerely hope they have a kennel large enough for Sam. I've heard it's cold in the cargo hold. Should I put him in his sweater?"

Raul rolls his eyes. "I'm sorry, but if you put that pussy sweater on him, I'm taking a different flight. Samson can tough it out like a real man."

"Says the gay man?" I'm smiling because Raul is always impeccably dressed and he can rock a sweater like no other man on earth.

His smirky face appears. "Oh, honey, if dick size makes the man, there isn't a *more* man than me."

"Argh, you're horrible. Use your muscle for something other than comedy and grab my bag. I'll get the leash."

We finally make it to the airport and all the doubts about my current predicament flood my brain. The airport is crowded and we stand in line while everyone gives us a wide berth because of Sam sitting at attention by my side. Finally, we make it to the check-in counter, where Mr. Mogul Dom's influence takes over. A small electric cart appears out of nowhere and an attendant ushers us on. I don't see a crate for Sam and ask about it. To my surprise, Sam is flying first class and has his own seat. I just hope he doesn't get airsick and barf all over me.

We bypass the long security line and head straight to the front. Sam passes through the metal detector with me and we're off again. This time our destination is the Admiral's Lounge. We settle in and enjoy an imported high-dollar beer that we don't pay for.

"I could grow accustomed to this very quickly," Raul comments after a long swallow of beer. I agree with him but I'll be damned if I say so.

Our flight is uneventful, if you don't count the fact that Samson wanted to sleep but couldn't get comfortable in his oversized seat. Finally, he was able to lie in the aisle and then he embarrassed me by snoring. Raul pretended he didn't know us.

Another cart picks us up at the gate and we speed along to a waiting limo. Carl takes our bags as soon as we're outside. "How was your flight, Ms. Simmons?"

"Fine, thank you," I say without smiling. "What should I call you?" I'm being as pleasant as possible and trying very hard not to show my dislike. Carl threw me into the car outside of the MC and I haven't forgiven him yet. Sadly, my Domme tendency to size up a man I would love to dominate comes into play. It's hard to ignore his thick neck and the muscles that bulge beneath his suit or the gorgeous bone structure of his face. I would love to have him on his knees with a leash attached to a collar around his throat. I wouldn't keep him for long but the fantasy of dominating him makes me feel better.

"Carl will do. It's a thirty minute drive to Club El Diablo and Mr. Collins wants you there as soon as possible."

"I was hoping I could go straight to my hotel." My bitchy grumble is loud and clear this time.

Carl ignores it. "Your suite is at The El Diablo. It's a luxury hotel and has everything you'll need. Mr. Collins wants to meet with you, but I don't think you'll be working tonight."

We take our seats in the limo and Sam, as usual, tries to sit on my lap. With a mighty heave, I shove him over. He's never figured out that he isn't a lap dog and he always manages to finagle at least half his body onto mine when I sit on the couch at home. The limo is no different in his opinion. I feel less defensive when Sam proceeds to drool and mess up the pristine leather seat. *Take that*, I silently cheer.

As promised, thirty minutes later we arrive at the hotel. The term "luxury" is an understatement. The outside fountains look like they come directly from the Bellagio in Vegas. The El Diablo is grand to the point of being ostentatious. Just the individual vehicles being valet parked cost more than the money I currently have in the bank and that's saying a lot after the cash Damian laid out.

Carl drives away and we follow another man inside—same build as Carl, same good looks, and the same demeanor. Why do the wealthy surround themselves with such extraordinary beauty? Ordinary looking people need jobs too. I'm one of those ordinary people and I'm walking into a job I don't want. Damn.

The inside of the hotel is just as riveting as the outside. For the next thirty days this will be my home. I inhale the smell of money. Anyone who thinks the rich and famous don't have an entirely different smell has never walked into a place like this.

"He's hot, rich, and eligible. You could do much worse," Raul whispers while we walk to the elevator.

"Shh, behave smartass. I'll wrap the man in a bow and deliver him to your room. I don't want him."

"Keep telling yourself that." We watch through the glass elevator as we travel to what appears to be the top floor.

"We're at the top?" I ask our escort.

"Almost. There is one more floor, but the only way to get there is to use one of Mr. Collins' private elevators.

Noticing the plural use of the word "elevators," I realize once more how far out of my depths I am. Damian Collins has it all and for the next thirty days I must resist being the fly to his creepy, crawly, highly deadly spider.

Our escort places a folded piece of expensive parchment paper in my hand. Five numbers boldly stare back at me.

"The access code for your rooms," he volunteers at my look of confusion.

I punch in the numbers and open the door. We enter a large foyer. Raul whistles with appreciation. From the highly polished marble beneath my feet to the incredible artwork on the walls, the suite is amazing. Samson sniffs out his new surroundings and I realize he needs a walk to take care of his business.

"Follow me, please," the escort says when I begin to voice my concern. We follow him through the cavernous rooms to a set of French doors. Stepping outside, sparkling lights show off an amazing outdoor oasis. The balcony wraps around the building and is about twelve feet wide. A four-foot wall separates the space from the Houston skyline. Real grass is under my feet, I can smell it.

"Mr. Collins assigned me and my co-worker to take Samson to the park when you're not available. Hotel staff will see to the dog waste deposited out here. I notified Mr. Collins of your arrival and he'll be here in a few minutes. Mr. Garcia, may I show you to your suite?"

My eyes meet Raul's. I know he won't leave if I want him here. I was hoping he would be sharing these rooms with me but apparently that isn't an option.

I give him my brave smile. "I'll be fine. Get settled and call me in an hour." He kisses my cheek and walks away. I know my eyes are impossibly large. "We are so *not* in Kansas anymore," I whisper to Sam, who is circling a spot on the grass.

I let him be and backtrack inside. I walk down a large hallway and peer into several rooms before locating the master suite. Sam arrives a few minutes into my exploration. There's another set of French doors in this room and Sam whines to be let out again. He needs to mark more territory. We walk outside and I stand at the balcony wall and look out over the city of Houston.

"I thought you might enjoy this view," the deep voice I've been dreading says from behind me.

I jump slightly and turn. Damian's dimples flash, causing me to inhale sharply. The man, who can instantly make my panties wet is wearing black sweatpants, running shoes, and nothing else. He is holding a bottle of water. A fine sheen of sweat coats his amazing chest. Damian isn't bulked muscle like his driver. His muscle is defined and lean, the plains and valleys showing off his six-pack abs to perfection. I want to lick each trail of sweat and bite his nipples. If only he were submissive, I could arrange a scene and get his body out of my mind by spending time on each square inch. He did this to me on purpose and his all-knowing smirk proves it. To top it off, I remember I forgot to pack my damn vibrator.

"Is the club here in the hotel?" I ask desperately so I don't just stand here and stare like an idiot.

He strides a few feet closer, causing my heartrate to accelerate. "So eager to begin working?" he asks in that slow, panty-melting drawl he's perfected.

I don't know what to do with my hands. I grab the wall with one and tuck the other into my side hoping Damian doesn't notice the trembling in my fingers. "Yes, the sooner I start, the sooner I can leave," I reply in my strict Domme voice.

He covers his heart with one hand. "You wound me, Mistress Lydia." He doesn't look wounded in the least. He's confident and oh so Domly.

Two can play this game. "Do you want me for your Mistress? I would love to use a bullwhip on your damp skin." I rub my palm against my skirt to show my anticipation.

His low and sexy laugh sizzles across my skin. My panties drench and he suddenly stops laughing as his eyes literally drip steam. This man plays havoc with my libido. "No," he says confidently. "My fantasy is you tied to my bed, legs spread, and your moans filling the room while my cock slides in and out of your delectable pussy."

His words throw a bucket of cold water on my elevated temperature. "That will remain your fantasy," I say with finality. "For a quarter of a million dollars, you might have talked me into whoring myself." My anger leaks through loud and clear. I have no idea why I allow him to get to me. He pulls my chain and I react. I need to reign myself in and give him a taste of his own medicine. That ability seems to leave the minute he's within ten feet of me.

"Tsk, tsk, Lydia." His eyes rake over my body with an intensity that makes me fidget like a newbie sub. "It isn't the money. I don't plan on paying for the use of your body when I know you'll willingly give it."

Damian obviously saw the lust I tried to hide and it only makes my resolve to keep him at arm's length that much stronger. "A good Dom respects a Domme and they don't feel the need to control *everyone*. You aren't the first Dom," I say the word "Dom" like it tastes bad, "to think he can flick a magical switch and make me into something I'm not."

"Is that what you think?" His dark eyes caress my body again. "I guarantee every man who watches you wield a whip wants you chained and screaming—Dom or sub it matters not." His gaze meets mine and heat swells between us. His voice lowers even further. "The difference is… I'm not intimidated by you and I go after what I want."

I gulp like a fool. "My body is not part of the deal." Even I don't believe my words. "You're making this job impossible for me and I haven't even started. I'm dominant and I won't sub for anyone."

He takes a step closer and like a fool, I step back.

He watches me closely. "You know if you use your little flip trick again I'll go over the wall, right?"

Finally, a chink in his armor. "That really got to you, didn't it?"

"Much more than you know and I still owe you a punishment, but not yet. I'll let you worry about it for a while longer. The anticipation should make you wetter."

I'm not going to lie. He knows women cream when he flashes those dimples, so I change the subject. "When do I start work?"

"Tomorrow night."

"Then I need my sleep." I want him out of here so I can pull myself together and come up with a game plan for dealing with him.

"A late night snack will be here in a moment." His damn eyes burn and he makes the mention of a snack sound sexy.

Samson heard the word snack and he comes running. He walks up to Mr. Wet Panty Advertisement and sniffs the hand Damian extends. He licks it once and then a second time.

I smile because Samson always calms me. "He likes the salt on your skin."

Damian gives me a side look and another slight grin. "I'd like you to lick the salt from my skin, but it's not my hand that's the saltiest."

Shivers run over every inch of skin on my body. "Does that line work on your other Dommes?"

"I don't want to fuck the other Dommes, and I'm afraid I never mix work with pleasure. When it comes to you I seem to bend all my rules."

"Poor me," I purr. "As the saying goes... get used to disappointment."

His eyes flare. "I don't usually care for ball gags, but I might make an exception with you."

"Is that a threat?" God, I hate him but I can't get the picture of licking his salty cock from my head.

He laughs again and doesn't bother answering. There's a soft chime from inside and Damian turns and walks back the way he came. Samson and I follow him around the outside of the apartment to the doors I entered when we first arrived.

Our waiter places the meal on a side table. After a short bow, he disappears. Damian pours wine like a pro. I look at the chair across from him and try to decide if holding onto my anger is worth missing out on the delicious smell coming from the tray. He cocks his eyebrows and patiently waits for me to make my decision. He uncovers a plate and slides it to my side of the table. Hell. I'm not made of steel. I take a bite while standing and I know immediately the cheese quesadilla was made in heaven. With a slight huff, I grudgingly take the offered chair.

"Room service and anything else you need is available using the house phone. Just press zero. Your phone is programmed to call my suite too." His dimples flash. "Just press 666."

I can't stop my return grin. The man is a marketing genius. Maybe I can learn something and make my forced thirty days working for him have meaning. "You take this entire devil thing very seriously."

He takes a drink of wine and nudges my glass. "It's my trademark and it's earned me a lot of money."

I lift my glass and sip. "I understand why you want me working at your club." I take another sip because it's damned good. "It's wanting me in your bed that I don't understand." The husky sound of my voice may have betrayed me.

Damian's expression turns serious. "I went to the Mediterranean already knowing what you looked like and how good you are as a Domme. I arrived just in time to see the tail end of your scene. I didn't expect my cock to respond. In this business, you become jaded. Watching a simple scene doesn't usually do it for me. On the contrary, I need to be vested in my own scene for my body to respond. There was something about seeing you work—your concentration and complete understanding of what your job truly is. It threw me for a loop and I haven't yet recovered. Even dressed as you are now in your loose flowing hippie clothes, I'm hard. I kept these sweatpants on because I knew I would be uncomfortable if I slipped on jeans." He rests his elbows on the table and his chin on his hands, which brings him closer to me. "Actually," he shakes his head, "I'm not sure what it is. You aren't the most beautiful woman I've met. You don't have the body I'm normally attracted to. But fuck, you're sexy as hell and I can't get you out of my head. I want your braid wrapped around my hand and your mouth on my cock. I want red stripes across your ass and thighs. Then I want to kiss each one with my fingers buried deep in your pussy. When you come, my mouth will be licking every bit of juice from between your thighs." The brown in his eyes goes darker the longer he talks.

I release a long sigh. Why did I ask such a stupid question? My ringing cell phone saves me. Fumbling with the phone, I finally manage to answer. "Umm, hello?" I take my eyes off Damian so I can think clearly.

The phone disappears from my hand. "She'll call you back in a few minutes." He disconnects the call with a flip of my archaic phone. Damian rises quickly from his chair. He doesn't touch me but bends his head and soft warm air blows past my ear when he speaks. "Your shift starts tomorrow night at nine. You have a newly filled closet of appropriate clothes. Carl will show you the way to the club. Be on time."

He steps back, leaves my phone on the table, and walks out the front door of the suite without looking back.

Chapter Ten

Damian

I'm a fool. I have no idea what it is about her. The last thing I should have done was lay all my cards on the table. I meant to keep things subtle and managed to blow that as soon as I saw her thanks to my hard dick. She brings out an intensity in me that I haven't felt in months. Hell, years.

I have no scenes scheduled tonight. Maybe I can catch up on paperwork. I enter my office and the first thing I notice is the folder that contains Lydia's background check. Against my better judgement, I flip through it again. The pictures do her no justice. I told the truth when I said she wasn't the most beautiful woman I know. She is the most striking, though. There's also something else I can't pinpoint and all I can do is re-read her file.

I'm reassured of one thing by the time I've read it again—Lydia has a gambling fetish. It's what made me offer her a wager in the first place. I never wager against something I can't win. Not her. She enjoys the endorphins winning against the odds releases. This doesn't help me at all, because I can't establish that special something that attracts me to her.

My desk phone rings, taking me away from thoughts of an infuriating redhead Domme. I pick it up and answer with my customary, "Damian."

"I'm surprised I caught you at your desk."

I immediately recognize the voice of my longtime friend Bran. I lay Lydia's file on my desk and relax back in my chair. "Me? All you do is work. Tell me you're headed this way and I'll line up the best subs we have."

His deep laugh fills the phone. "The workload hasn't lightened up. You should also know I've turned over a new leaf and I've given up my darker side." Bran has always considered BDSM his darker side and not his true lifestyle. "I hope this won't affect our friendship?"

Now my laughter takes over. "No, you son of a bitch, that will never happen. I'd need to bust your nose again if it did." I don't mention that what he's trying to do is near impossible. Bran is a Dom through and through.

"So tell me you have some sweet young sub that's changed your love 'em and leave 'em policy?"

Now I have an inkling of what the problem is. Bran wants to settle down. He wouldn't ask me about sticking with one sub if he didn't want exactly that for himself. An image of Lydia flashes through my mind.

"There's someone," Bran states emphatically. "You're too slow in answering. Well shit, it's about time."

This is not the impression I want him to have. Lydia is a passing fancy only. "No commitments at the moment. There is a young Domme giving me problems. She's… different."

"Different," Bran breathes into the phone. "And a Domme? Maybe I'm reading something unusual into this conversation that isn't there. You're talking club issues?"

"Hell." I pull my fingers through my short hair in frustration. "A club issue and an attitude issue leaving me with a perpetually hard dick."

"Whoa. Are you treading on the sub side of things?"

Now I stand and pace my office. "Hell no, though if I were, my problems with Lydia would most likely be solved."

"I look forward to meeting this bombshell. It'll need to be outside the club, though. I'm a new man."

I chuckle. "Afraid of your willpower if you visit?"

His return laugh is full of derision. "I'm on step one of the kink twelve-step program."

"What, pray tell is step one?"

"Self-denial," he replies.

"Fuck, I wouldn't stand a chance."

Chapter Eleven

Lydia

I stand admiring Raul's closet full of BDSM attire. His leathers come with a small pitchfork emblem. Mine do not. Raul choses a set of clothes for his first night of work that shows off his nearly perfect physique. The outfit also exposes his ass cheeks. I knew about the scars on his hip and upper leg from a motorcycle accident when he was a teenager. He usually hides the marred skin but with his choice of outfits, the scars are a statement and make him sexier if that's possible.

"Do you think they'll fire me the first night for frightening the customers?" he asks while taking a final look over his shoulder in the mirror.

My hands twitch over the need to dominate him and add a few marks to his sexy ass. "We're both walking away if they do, but I've always told you your scars are exciting and they made me want to soothe you that first night I chose you for a sub."

Raul huffs out a breath and smiles. "Still one of my best memories. Tell me why we became friends and you no longer top me?"

I smile back. "Because you are much better as my assistant than you ever were as my slave. You cry too easy."

He chuckles. "Keep it up and I'll find some big bad Dom tonight and leave you alone with Master D."

"So it's Master D now?"

"Well, you never use the same endearment twice and that man can master me anytime he wants. I hear he doesn't bang the staff. What a shame." He winks. "You're blushing," he points out. "This should be a fun night."

I refuse to acknowledge his teasing. "Let me dress and then we'll get this disaster over with."

I head back to my suite. The wardrobe selection I have is far more extensive than Raul's and the closet itself is the size of my bedroom back home. There's a mirrored wall and a white plush bench in the middle of the vast room—all of it mine for thirty days and I should make the most of the time I have. I select a black leather front lace-up corset. There's a purple ruffle at the top that does little to hide the swell of my breasts. My nipples will most likely spill out at some point during the night. I also choose a black leather skirt that laces up the sides. I have an inch of skin showing down the center of the top and down the sides of the skirt. Rarely do I leave my pussy bare when I work, but tonight I don't bother with panties. It's time to live a little and I doubt I need to be worried about a police raid like I did at the MC.

My black boots back home were cheap and uncomfortable. I slip on a pair of four-inch supple leather ankle boots from the closet and fall in love. They fit like a dream. I guess my background check included shoe size.

I don't go for garish makeup, but I do add black eyeliner with slight swirls at the sides. My eyes are a deep green and one of my best features. My hair is in its customary braid, this one high on my head. With a touch of deep red lipstick, I'm ready. *NOT*.

My hands shake when I open the door after hearing a soft knock. Raul and Carl stand waiting. Raul's whistle makes me blush.

His eyes travel over my ensemble several times. "Wow, Chiquita, I so want to play."

"It's Mistress to you," I snap in my Domme voice. It's time for the show and I won't take any shit from Raul for the rest of the night. He knows I won't discipline him but I have no problem finding someone who will.

"Yes, Mistress." I hear the smile in his voice, the jerk.

I turn to Carl. "Are my personal items set up?"

"Yes," he replies and I arch an eyebrow.

Raul answers next. "I made sure everything is the way you like but my work was overseen, Mistress." His voice now holds a touch of disgruntlement, which I ignore. Now is not the time nor place for an open discussion about Damian's spying.

"Let's do this," I say with a flick of my braid. I'll never really be ready for tonight and I just want it over with. Or at least that's how a part of me feels. The other half, that dominant part that pushes at me, is more than ready. I need to let off a little steam and my hands itch to feel a whip within their grasp.

We follow Carl. He leads us away from the bank of elevators we took the evening before and stops at what looks like another guest room door or maybe even a linen closet. Carl enters a PIN number and the door opens. An elevator door slides quietly to the side.

"Use your private suite code for this elevator and it will take you directly to the club. You may go there when you're not working. If you want a non-kinky atmosphere, use the lobby or second floor bars. There's also an indoor pool and health club. Your room will have a list of everything the hotel offers. Use your room number on the bar or dining tab; everything is paid under the terms of your contract."

Carl says all this during the elevator ride. The door slides open and the world changes to a kinky wonderland. The lighting is low with spotlights accenting scene alcoves. The sounds of spanking and cries are normal for the BDSM scene, but that's where normal stops.

There is a real, honest to God carousel in the center of the large rotunda. It circles slowly with subs riding brightly colored horses. Some have their hands bound to the pole in front of them while others just hold on. Colorful lights glow and turn a child's ride into an erotic wonderland. There's a spanking bench, no two, where the customary benches would be on a normal carousel. It's totally awesome, erotic, and out of this world. This is a true BDSM playground.

A young male sub is on one of the spanking benches, displayed in all his glory, and having his ass striped pink by a Domme. I watch the scene play out in spinning increments. My nerves settle. I'm back in my element.

I finally tear my eyes away from the carousel and glance around at more signs of over-the-top wealth. There's a large bar area off to the left that includes tables and chairs with a grand piano, giving it a lounge feel. Three employees handle drink orders from behind the bar while waitresses take orders from the guests at the tables. The men are dressed in black, silk, long-sleeved shirts completely opened down the front with black bowties identifying them as El Diablo employees. The female employees have lacy black bras beneath the shirts and skintight leather skirts.

A woman is lying face down on top of the bar and whenever a Dom sitting nearby places an order, they deliver a hard slap to her naked behind. Her shoulders are shaking and a small sob escapes her with each blow. Bad sub.

The scenes may be similar to what happens at the Mediterranean Club but there's no comparison when it comes to the wealth and class of Club El Diablo. I'm startled when a warm hand lands on my arm. Turning, I barely manage to breathe. Damian's chest is bare and smooth. His six-pack melts into leather pants that look painted on. They disappear into black leather boots that stop just below his knees. Each muscled valley begs to be explored. I barely have enough control to keep my hands off. Slowly, my eyes travel back to his face.

Dimples.

Twinkling eyes.

Scruffy jaw that makes me grip my hands into a fist to keep from reaching out and running my fingers across his chin. He releases my arm and surprisingly, I'm able to stand on my own. Even in full Domme mode, it's pure torture to be around him.

"Mistress Lydia." His warm hand captures mine and he slowly raises it to his lips and kisses the inside of my wrist. Heat flares. His tongue flicks out and licks the same place he kissed. My pussy clenches and it takes everything I have to stay standing and not drop to my knees. How does he do this to me in mere seconds?

"I'd like to show you around and I also have a surprise." His thick voice draws me away from some very wicked thoughts that do not mesh with my Domme status.

"That would be wonderful," I reply in an embarrassingly breathy voice. I must gain control of myself. He leads me closer to the carousel.

"If you choose a sub for the night, they can wait on the carousel if you need to leave them alone. House rules keep Doms from using another's sub without permission. You can also see that public discipline is one of the carousel's best features."

I notice the sub flogged only moments ago. His mouth works between the Domme's thighs while she holds tight to a pole. Many Doms and Dommes expect pleasure from their subs. I gain satisfaction through the domination itself. I hand out orgasms as a gift to my subs and I'm fulfilled when they are.

"You also need to understand the significance of the gold heart bracelets and necklaces. Inside the club, we have color wrist bands to designate preferences and kink experience. Outside these walls, subs wear the gold hearts so they're easily identified by kinky visitors to the hotel. The kink community stays on the top five floors but all lounges and restaurants are open for non-kinky pursuits. Above all else we offer privacy for our guests and ask that vanilla only conversations take place when on the lower floors."

My gaze leaves Damian when the slow spinning of the carousel stops and a young woman steps down. She approaches us with a very familiar sexy walk. I swear my heart stalls. It's Angela dressed in an El Diablo employee uniform. She goes to her knees at my feet. I reach down and reverently touch her hair. Warmth travels up my arm and through my body with the connection.

"Permission to speak, Mistress?"

"Yes, Angela, you have permission." Tears burn my eyes.

"I arrived this morning. Master D gave me a job and when I'm not working, I'm a full member of the club."

A frown replaces my tender smile. "You traveled this morning and you're working tonight?"

"Yes, Mistress, but Master D told me if I didn't take a nap I could not come in this evening. He wanted me here so you would feel more comfortable. I would like to write myself on your schedule for next week if it pleases you, Mistress?"

Damian is manipulating me again but there's no way I would take that out on Angela. I left a message on her phone before I left California explaining that I was leaving for a month. I never heard back and I've been incredibly worried about her. "Yes, it pleases me, Angela. Thank you for making my evening brighter."

She looks so happy staring up at me. "Thank you, Mistress, I must get back to work."

I help her stand. "Yes, you should. I'm not sure kneeling while you're on duty is a good idea."

Damian's voice interrupts. "I don't mind. She asked and I granted her this small favor."

I stop Angela with a slight touch to her arm. She turns and I gently kiss her cheek. "Thank you for being here."

"Yes, Mistress." Angela gives me an amazingly sweet smile before she strolls away.

"Do you like my surprise?"

I fight the desire to push him to the floor and fuck his brains out. "Your control of my life makes me nervous," I answer honestly and hope he doesn't read the need in my eyes.

"Too bad. You lost the bet." He smiles wickedly. "We need to finish your tour."

"You cheated." I say with a disgruntled huff that Mr. Nasty Nipples ignores. I inhale slowly and gain control of my unfulfilled body.

Curious eyes follow us. Damian takes in everything with a sweeping gaze but for the most part ignores the patrons. The entire club is lavish and even smells delicious—leather, wood oil, and sex—

nothing like the Mediterranean. Everything looks new, expensive, and clean. The lighting is perfect and the music in the background subtle with a heavy bass. A group of kinksters sit on low couches playing cards in the lounge. Subs kneel at their feet—some naked and others barely clothed. This is the world of pleasure and money—my world for a short time.

What surprises me most is everyone is *not* beautiful with artificially enhanced body parts. There's a pretty, pleasantly plump woman wearing the collar of her Dom. He hands her a drink and sweetly touches her hair. She smiles and thanks him by kissing his palm.

There's an older couple—both look to be in their sixties. He's collared, at the knees of his Domme and appears blissfully happy, gray hair and all.

"Excuse me, Master D," a man says. "We have a matter that needs your attention." The man is dressed in a club uniform.

Damian glances my way. "Come with me, please." He holds out his arm for me to precede him.

I so want to *come* but I think we're on two different pages here. My thoughts have nothing to do with following anyone. I want Damian's cock buried deep in my pussy when it happens. I hide my need again, nod, and follow the employee. Loud sobs can be heard as we approach a station in the back corner of the main room.

The employee isn't happy. "Master Ellis was escorted out. His sub has a few bruises and he didn't stop when she used her safe word. I'll have his file on your desk in the morning, but I thought you might want to see to Melody yourself, Sir."

Damian's anger is palpable and I don't miss the tight fists he makes at his sides. He enters the alcove separated from the play area by lush plants. I can smell the rich soil of the greenery and know they're real. A woman is lying on the couch with a blanket wrapped around her. Damian sits beside her. "Are you okay, Melody?" he asks.

"He hurt me." She sniffs. "I used my safe word but he wouldn't stop."

"Do you need medical attention?" He tilts her face up so she's looking directly at him while they speak.

"No, Master D. I'll be okay."

"I'm glad. Here, sit in my lap." He pulls her gently over and cradles her like a baby. The blanket slips and her bare upper body is displayed. Damian's hand presses her head against his shoulder and then goes to her breast. He kneads the plump flesh tenderly. His other hand pushes the blanket lower and finds her shaved pussy. He massages her labia with practiced fingers.

Fuck me. My gut clenches and my fingernails dig into the skin on my thighs. I'm jealous. I've watched this happen with subs hundreds of times and I have gentled subs in this same manner. Why do I want this man's hands on me and only me? The longing grows worse when Damian kisses her. It's tender and sweet and I want Melody to disappear in a cloud of smoke so I can take her place.

"Stephen, please have Melody's preferred drink delivered here and find Kyle for me."

"Yes, Sir."

I continue to watch while Mr. Lusty Master comforts the now quiet and content female.

"You called, Master D?" Kyle says.

He's tall, almost the size of Damian, and he's incredibly gorgeous. I would have a tough time deciding who is better looking. This hunk isn't dressed as an employee. He's pure Dom.

"Do you have a sub for the night, Kyle?"

"No, I don't."

"Melody has need of a little TLC and I'm hoping you can take her to one of the private rooms and make her feel better."

Kyle gives me a quick glance before he turns his gaze to the woman on Damian's lap. "My pleasure. I take it Master Ellis will not be returning?"

I'm surprised steam isn't pouring from Damian's eyes. His jaw clenches tight but his hands on Melody are tender. "No, he won't be back. Could I also ask you to watch over Melody until a new Dom can be found for her?"

"Again, my pleasure." He smiles at Melody, whose eyes are large and apprehensive.

"Master Kyle will be gentle with you. He will make sure you have someone who will always honor your safe word."

Melody sighs in what I can only take as relief. I give Kyle another look. Reading between the lines, I'm guessing Kyle likes things rough. I like him more for taking on Melody when she's not his type.

Damian looks at me but speaks to Kyle. "I'm sure you've figured out at that this is Mistress Lydia. And just so you know," Damian's eyes go dark and his voice deeper, "she's off limits except to the subs."

What? Did I just hear him right?

Kyle smiles and takes my hand much like Damian did earlier. He lifts my fingers to his mouth but a glare from Mr. Dramatic stops him before he places his lips on me. Kyle grins and tips his chin down in acknowledgment. "It's nice to me you, Mistress Lydia."

"Nice to meet you, Master Kyle." He drops my hand and I can't help myself. My fingers grab his and I raise them to my lips. My tongue comes out.

Kyle quirks his eyebrows at me and follows it with a wink. He then lifts Melody from Mr. Control Freak's arms and walks away.

"You will be punished for that too, my dear."

"Promises promises." I bite my lip so I don't smile.

I glance down at his crotch where his erection strains against the leather. "I see Melody has you hot and bothered?"

So suddenly he catches me by surprise; Damian's arms wrap around me and his lips take mine. They nibble, they suck, and then when I start to push him away, they devour. My pussy goes into overdrive and my pelvic bone rocks against his hard cock. His hand goes to my braid and uses it to tug my head back, giving his mouth better access. His tongue thrusts deep while his hands hold me firmly in place. He's in control and I'm nothing but a weak kitten.

After I'm thoroughly kissed—hot, bothered, and wet—his lips end their assault. His chin rests on the top of my head and he speaks with a throaty growl. "We can't do this here. It's bad for business and bad for you in general." His hand tightens in my hair. "Come to bed with me when your shift is over. We need to get this out of our systems. I need to fuck you." He turns slightly and whispers in my ear, "Say yes."

I fill my lungs with his musky scent. The soap he uses and the spicy man-mix are incredibly erotic. I exhale. "Sorry, but I decline and I would prefer you not kiss me again." I'm glad he can't see my lie. "I'm not sleeping with you and I don't care if I'm in your system or not. I have sex on my own terms and my private life belongs to me. I might want to fuck you but I won't. Candy is not good for my teeth or hips."

His chuckle is low and rich. "You are so damn stubborn. I want your teeth on my candy." He grinds his erection against me once before releasing me so he can see my eyes. "I promise my cum is sweeter than chocolate and you can lick it up." His dimples are in full on sexy mode.

I shake my head at his ridiculousness. "You did not just say that."

He touches the skin of my throat and draws his thumb across my wanting flesh. "I want to make you laugh and talk dirty to you while you come. I want…"

"Stop." My hand covers his mouth and the son of a bitch bites me. It's not a gentle nip either. "Ouch." I pull my hand away. I've got to bring this back around to the work at hand. "Okay Mr. Fuck Fangs, I'd like to explore your club and get to work, but I need a sub. I'd also appreciate a recommendation. Tonight I want a male. He needs to be tall, with dark hair and eyes. Some heavy muscle would also be nice. If you have a twin brother, I'll take him."

Damian gives a robust laugh. I hate to admit to enjoying the sound. I also hate how sexy laughter is on him.

"Your wish is my command, and I have the perfect sub for you."

Oh, I just bet he does.

Holly S. Roberts

Chapter Twelve

Damian

The moment I saw Lydia tonight my dick went hard. Her tight ass in the leather, barely there skirt, and the shimmy of skin at her hips and belly only made me crazier. Hell, she's still driving me nuts. I brought her little subby here to help ease the way. Seeing Angela kneel at Lydia's feet only intensified my hard-on.

Then I tasted Lydia's sweet lips. The kiss said I was getting someplace with her. The way she kissed me back said she wasn't as averse to me as she pretends. I kiss subs to settle and comfort them. It's a technique that usually works for both sub and Dom. Kissing is personal and helps form a bond during a scene. I find enjoyment in it. I love the taste of women. What happened with Lydia is almost indescribable. Her taste is different and I have a feeling the residue of the kiss will make every kiss from here on out unacceptable.

I also notice the way she looks at me when she thinks I'm not watching. Raw hunger is the only way to describe it, and I shouldn't be happy we're both suffering from whatever it is that seems to be pulling us together. I don't need to look in a mirror to know my eyes hold the same need as hers.

I run my fingers through my short hair. Lydia messes with my senses and I need to pull my head out of my ass and get some paperwork done. I enter my office and take a seat behind my large oak desk. I stare at the stack of invoices I need to sign and all I really see is a fantasy flash of Lydia bending over the desk and showing me her tight little asshole.

The image changes and a mental glimpse of Lydia with Adam, the sub I recommended, pops into my thoughts. I angrily pull the top invoice closer and look over the order.

Lydia purposefully asked for a sub fitting my description. She did it to drive me fucking crazy. Sadly, I admit defeat because she did fucking win. Adam isn't a threat, but right now I'd like to kick his ass out of the club.

My thoughts are totally wrong. I know they are and it doesn't stop them. I sign and review five orders before I can no longer stand not seeing what Lydia is up to. How pathetic can she make me?

I leave my office and enter the main section of the club. I need to check in with the front office and make sure everything is running smoothly. I also need to get my head back on straight, but the crowd forming around the St. Andrew's Cross clues me in that the woman keeping me from sanity is at work. Yeah, my cock twitches again and I move closer.

Adam is tied to the cross. Lydia, her skin glowing with a fine sheen of sweat, is working him over with a four-foot whip. She's good with it and checks her surroundings before each strike. When she lifts her arm, her top pulls tightly across her breasts and I can see her pert nipples straining beneath the fabric.

I remain behind the crowd while the scene plays out. Adam is nearing his limit and I'm impressed that Lydia reads him so well. He has a habit of requesting more pain than he actually wants. Lydia lays down the whip and begins rearranging the cross with Raul's help. After the cross is flat and Adam is facing upright, Lydia lifts her skirt to her waist. I'm unsurprised she's bare beneath the material. She uses a top bar to hold herself up while she straddles the cross and Adam's mouth eats her pussy.

Fuck but the look on her face while Adam works is almost more than I can take. I don't even realize I'm moving forward. Onlookers step aside and I'm standing about five feet away. Lydia doesn't notice me. Her eyes are mostly closed with pleasure lighting up her face. It won't take Adam much to send her over. She's so fucking responsive and somehow I need to stop thinking of her as a sub. Lydia is a dominant who knows what she wants. I'm mentally invested in the scene when Lydia's facial muscles tighten. My gaze travels down to her pussy and I catch the slightest trembling of her legs as her orgasm rolls through her body. Yes, I'd like to be Adam right now, but the view I have shouldn't be missed. Lydia's beauty multiplies as she freely gives the crowd her orgasm.

Her eyes gradually open and she's staring straight at me. I slowly reach down and her gaze follows my movement. I place my hand on the outside of my leathers wishing the damn things were made of cotton so I could take relief. I press firmly against the hardness of my cock and slide my hand from balls to tip.

Lydia licks her lips, and like a fucking teenager, I almost come in my damn pants.

Holly S. Roberts

Chapter Thirteen

Lydia

Adam is a hot cowboy. He's no Damian, but I won't complain. I'm so fucking horny I could ride one of the carousel horses and get off in two seconds flat. Adam's hat and chaps are sexy. His body beneath them even sexier. I worried that Mr. Fuck Me Tonight would give me a complete loser. It's nice to be wrong. Adam will give me what I need. In my mind, his mouth, tongue, and teeth will be Damian's.

A crowd gathers at the entrance to the alcove while I strap Adam to a St. Andrew's Cross. This one is top of the line and can be positioned to lie flat, which will be perfect for later.

I step up close and go to my tiptoes once I have Adam secured facing out with his back to the cross. "Your safe word?" I whisper knowing my hot breath in his ear adds to the sensations he's feeling right now.

"Red, Mistress." The tremor in his words sings to my heart.

Fear is half the fun of working with a new sub. "We've discussed limits. I know you like pain and I'll give you a touch, but tonight we're becoming familiar with each other. Understood?"

"Yesss, Mistress," he breathes out erratically. I've seen subs like him before. The scared rabbit in his eyes gives him away. He can't take the pain I could inflict.

I kiss him. This isn't like Damian's kiss. It doesn't consume me or set fire to my blood. It eases Adam's fear just a bit, which is what I intend. Not too much, though.

Standing, I remove a cock ring from a tray on the side table and clamp it on his erection. He groans and I smile. The ring will trap the blood in his cock and make the wait for release agonizing.

"Shh, don't make a sound or you won't like the punishment."

I use a four-foot braided whip. It's new leather, I can smell it. I warm up my wrist and snap the whip a few times. Adam sucks in a sharp breath and I smile again while my mind drifts to the deep dark place I crave. This is my own special universe where I can block out everything around me and concentrate on my sub.

Adam trembles harder when I run my hands across his chest and then over his firm hip. I kiss him again and his heartbeat picks up beneath my hand. I move my fingers down to his cock and I run them along the metal of the ring, clicking my fingernails so he feels and hears the sounds. His breathing accelerates delightfully while mine remains slow and steady.

"Shh, remember my command."

He knows better than to speak. I step away and release the short coil. It drops to the floor and I rotate my wrist one last time. The crowd goes completely quiet.

I raise my hand and flick the whip. Just the tip hits Adam's thigh and his entire body jumps. I give him only enough time to inhale before I strike his leg very close to his engorged cock. He breathes out an unintelligible word, which is a no-no. I step in close and squeeze his balls hard enough to cause a loud grown.

"You know better, Adam. Silence unless you're using your safe word," I demand in my deepest Domme voice. I don't usually require silence, but Adam's voice is nothing like Damian's and I don't want him ruining my fantasy. I've never treated a sub this way and by that I mean as a substitute for someone else. I'll make it up to Adam, I promise myself, but right now I need him for one purpose only.

I increase the speed of my strikes and give Adam little time to gather himself between the burning lashes. Tears roll down his face. I pay close attention and stop before he completely panics. Someone needs to speak with Adam about changing his limits. Angela can handle more than he can. It's only a problem for me because it's dangerous for Adam. I'm willing to use him again but there will be a very serious talk before it happens. I enjoy choosing my scene partners according to my desires. Adam will not make a good whipping post on nights when I need a heavy workout. Adam definitely has other uses, though, and I plan to take advantage of them.

My body is slick with sweat. I walk to the controls of the cross and loosen the turn wheels that allow me to lower the cross horizontally. Raul helps and the well-oiled joints glide smoothly into place. I walk around so I'm at the head of the cross and I slide my skirt up past my hips. I don't look at the crowd because right now it's all about what Adam's about to do for me.

There's a bar positioned above Adam and I grab it, turn around, and sink down so Adam knows exactly what I want. "Lick me. Slowly. Clean my pussy."

My head goes back at the first flick of his tongue. "Fuck yes," I groan. I grind up and down on his mouth. I move slightly so his nose hits my clit. My orgasm builds. I close my eyes while imagining only one mouth on my cunt, one tongue licking and sucking me. I picture Damian's face, his grin, and those sexy dimples. The orgasm pulses through my pussy and I cry out. Yes, I will be using Adam again. I hope he remains unattached and doesn't find a steady Domme.

Slowly, I open my eyes. Burning dark orbs pierce me. My sexual release has barely ended and I feel it spike again. It's Damian's scalding gaze. He's watching me intently. If I didn't know better, I would think him jealous. I slowly back off Adam, lean down, and kiss him. Take that Mr. Palatial Penis.

I stand straight and pull my skirt back down without looking toward Damian. Raul helps me re-adjust the cross so Adam is upright again and I remove the cock ring. Adam groans but manages to hold most of the sound in, which brings another smile to my lips.

"It's okay now," I assure him. "This is for you. If it feels good, I want to hear it." I run my fingers over the side of his face and receive a relieved smile.

I remove a cherry flavored condom from the tray beside me and roll it over Adam's cock. I like candy and this kind has no calories. I work my tongue over him and then take him fully into my mouth. Damian is bigger. It was obvious when he ran his hand over his erect cock. I suck and tease while massaging his balls with one hand. Adam's cries grow louder and finally he shouts his release.

I don't need to look to know Damian is no longer around. The thrill of having him watch is no longer tingling up my spine. I look anyway. He's gone. I unbuckle the leather cuffs from Adam's legs first. Raul unstraps his wrists and asks Adam if he can stand on his own. A ripple of applause travels through the crowd before they move along.

Raul assists Adam to a couch hidden by a grouping of plants that covers the alcove behind the scene area. The posh club has a small alcove behind each station for aftercare.

I sit down and pat my lap so Adam puts his head on my thighs. I pull a soft blanket over his nude body. "Raul, can you get us bottled water?" I smooth Adam's hair back.

"Yes, Mistress," Raul answers.

"Tell me about yourself, Adam."

And it begins. Adam starts talking and within a few minutes he's crying. He wants to be controlled but he admits he doesn't enjoy severe pain. This is information I can work with. Adam's last Dom left him because of his pain intolerance issues. Hell, I've had subs who couldn't handle pain at all. Everyone is different. I make sure Adam understands the fault is not his. If he wants a permanent Dom or Domme, he needs to be honest about his hard limits.

"Are you looking for a permanent sub?" he asks me shyly.

I kiss his cheek to soften my refusal. "I'm here for a month and would be happy to work with you on a limited basis. When the month is up, we won't see each other again. I would be happy to help you chose someone permanent if you like."

"Thank you, Mistress."

Raul returns with water and I comfort Adam for another thirty minutes to assure myself he's okay. "Adam, would you be willing to finish showing me around? I'll buy you a drink."

"I'd be honored, Mistress." He puts his chaps and hat back on his gorgeous body.

Raul strolls up to me when we leave the scene area. "Will you be staying past your shift?" I ask him.

"Yes, Mistress. I have a Dom interested in me. I have another hour of work tonight and then I'll go up to my room and change if you don't mind."

"Have fun."

"I plan to." He gives me a wink and walks away.

I glance at Adam. "I would like to meet some of the other Doms and Dommes. Are there any you think I would like?"

"Mistress Anna is a favorite and so is Master Jordan. He likes fire play and he should be at his station soon. It's always a big show."

"I'm not into fire play myself, but I wouldn't mind watching. Lead the way, please." I notice a large crowd a few stations down. "Is that the fire play station?" I nod to the alcove attracting the attention.

"No, Mistress, fire play is only performed at station five. You're looking at station three."

"Let's see what's going on." We walk over and the crowd is so thick it's hard to see what's happening in the scene. Adam is taller than I am and I glance up and see a look of pure bliss cross his face. I can't help wondering if this is the Dom who left him.

I squeeze in between two men in front of us and inhale sharply when I see what all the fuss is about. It's Damian in full Dom mode, and fuck is he sexy. The large butt plug in his hand makes me squirm. He has a woman draped over a spanking bench. She's writhing and moaning loudly. He separates her ass cheeks while massaging the plump orbs. Her body is lush and beautiful. She's not one of the wafer thin subs that I expected him to work with.

It hits me. The sub has red hair and a similar body to mine. Damian is paying me back in spades. A scream rings out from the sub when Damian runs the butt plug along the crack of her ass. She is behaving badly and the damn thing isn't even inserted.

Damian slaps his hand down hard across her ass.

"I don't mind hearing you scream when I give you a reason, but I've barely touched you."

"I'm afraid, Master."

"I think I can help with that, but I want silence for the next five minutes, understood?"

"Yes, Master."

Fuck, fuck, fuckity fuck. He's semi-imitating my scene.

His finger enters her pussy. He adds another. I can hear the wetness of her cunt as his fingers drill in and out. It's slow torture to watch and I clench my thighs. Her rounded ass bucks slightly when he increases his tempo, but she remains mostly quiet.

With every fiber of my body in need of Damian, the scene strikes a chord and I realize how Damian felt while he watched me. I. Want. To. Be. His. Sub. Someone kill me now. My fucking cunt throbs. Turning to Adam, I nod to the floor. He doesn't question me and simply sinks to his knees. I press his head to my hip in a loving gesture. "Watch." I want his eyes on the scene and not on me. I have a feeling I give too much away when it comes to Master D.

When the woman's orgasm starts, Damian inserts the plug in her ass and Miss Screams A Lot lets loose. It's an irritating high-pitched cry, but I guess some men like it. Oh, Lydia, thy name is jealousy. I smile and at that moment, Damian looks straight into my eyes. His ignite and I return his gaze with answering flames before I can stop myself.

Damn. I can't get away fast enough. Poor Adam has trouble coming off his knees and keeping up as my fast stride carries me as far away from the scene as I can get. I could take Adam to an alcove and do another scene, but I need to control myself. I cannot allow Damian to win this round.

Hell. He already has.

Over the next few hours, I speak to several Doms and Dommes. They pay membership dues and look at me as something of an oddity. Apparently Club El Diablo has never paid for a Dom or Domme. These people are rich on a level I've never seen and most likely will never know. They don't seem stuck on their social status, though. Yes, they're dominant, but along with that they have the same insecurities I've seen in myself.

People may think dominants are secure in who they are and in many ways they're correct. But not in everything. There is a lot of pressure in looking out for needy people. From the corner of my eye, I catch Damian walking from scene to scene and checking in on his clients. He worries. I saw it in his expression when he cared for the abused sub earlier. There's a lot of weight stacked on Damian's shoulders.

He's an excellent Dom. At the Mediterranean Club they were few and far between. Banning a Dom from that club was almost unheard of. Slide a little money across Johnny Ford's palm and any lines you've crossed disappear. I approve of Damian's ethics. Honestly, I approve of everything about Damian but his ability to soak my non-existent panties and his inability to take me off his sub radar.

"He's scrumptious," Anna says when Damian walks by. Her comment pulls me out of my thoughts of the big bad Dom.

"If I liked the arrogant, pushy type, I'd agree with you."

Anna is one of the Dommes Adam introduced me to. I really like her and we have plans for shopping later in the week. She gives me a sharp look but doesn't argue with my assessment. Like most good Dommes, she misses little and I have no idea if I fooled her.

We make solid plans for our shopping trip and say our goodbyes. It's after two a.m. and I'm exhausted. Adam scheduled with me for the following week before he left. He was a fountain of information and gave me the lowdown on several subs he thought I might enjoy. He also told me more about his poor little rich boy life. Again, Damian was right—money *can* fuck you up. At least Adam seems stable now and he's working on his master's degree in psychology. Too bad I will be long gone when he starts practicing.

I make it back to my suite and let Samson outside. Once we're settled, I fall to sleep and dream of Damian's mouth doing deliciously dirty things to me.

Holly S. Roberts

Chapter Fourteen

Damian

Keeping my eyes off Lydia throughout the long night wasn't easy. I walked by the group she spent most of the evening with several times and covertly checked in to be sure she was okay. She appeared comfortable in her surroundings and at home with the other Masters and Mistresses of the club. Adam stayed close, which caused my teeth to grind. I should have given her someone old enough to be her grandfather.

Hell, I walked face first into her demand for a sub who looks like me. The redhead I chose didn't come close to sating my lust for her, though. I'm tired, accomplished very little tonight, and I'm not in the best of moods. My apartment on the floor above Lydia's is silent and empty. I haven't had a long-time sub staying here in a while. Maybe my problem is loneliness.

As if the one constant woman in my life can read my thoughts, my cell rings. It's almost three in the morning and only one person would call at this time.

"Hi, Mom," I answer.

"Oh good you're awake," she replies cheerfully. "I hope I'm not disturbing you and your future wife."

I roll my eyes. We've been down this road too many times to count. I almost give my usual answer of, "Someday, maybe, but not now." I think about Lydia and answer honestly, "No, unfortunately you didn't. Maybe you'll get lucky another night."

Silence.

"You there, Mom?"

"You found someone?" There is so much hope in her voice. I'm her only child and she wants mountains of grandkids to spoil rotten.

"Her name is Lydia. The problem is she's not exactly happy I found her."

"Psh," she makes a disgusted sound into the phone. "You have your father's charm. She'll come around. Let me know if you need me there to help convince her."

I can't stop my grin because she's deadly serious. "I don't think that will be necessary. She's stubborn and I just need to work on those charm skills you're talking about."

"A minimum of three grandchildren is what I want, so do whatever you need to make it happen."

The mental image of Lydia with a nice round belly pops into my head and I almost groan aloud. "Duly noted."

"Tell me about her."

So I do. My mother is fully aware of Club El Diablo and what it is. She's not shy about talking sex and I know she has a kinky background, I just refuse to listen to her talk about it. Yes, there is an ick factor involved and I feel uncomfortable but Mom does not.

"You tricked her and now she's angry. Good job, Damian Joseph Collins."

I run my fingers across my head. She's really pulling out the big guns by using my full name. "I'll make it right. Trust me on this."

She chuckles into the phone. "I have no doubts about that. It's nice to know you've met your match. I'd rather see her give you a run for your money than instantly fall into your lap. Now it's time for me to go back to reading my romance novel so I can get some sleep. You need to rest too. Good night, son."

"Good night, Mom."

I look around the apartment. It's still as quiet, but talking to my mother takes a bit of the lonely out of it. I can picture Lydia here. The picture includes her on her knees. Christ, my dick goes hard again. A hot shower and quick hand job help take the edge off. After that, I somehow manage to sleep like a baby.

***

My cell rings again a little after six. There's no name attached to the number but I recognize it.

"Damian," I answer in a foggy, sleep-deprived voice.

"I need you in two hours," Monroe's clipped tone charges into my ear.

"Where?" I ask as I sit up in bed and try to gather my wits.

"I'll text the information. I have three women. Can you handle it?"

Three is doable. "Yes, I can handle it," I assure him.

The call ends and I call my mom. She doesn't seem nearly as tired as I am.

"You know I'll make room for three."

Yes, I do. She'll also be the best thing that ever happened to these women. "Thank you, Mom. I'll see you in a few hours."

Monroe sends a follow-up text and gives me a destination that will require the helicopter. I call the emergency pilot because I haven't scheduled a flight. We take off an hour later. A car picks me up from the airport and I'm driven to a quiet area with neat houses in rows.

Monroe greets me with a subtle head nod. He's a genius and a man of few words. He's not partial to handshakes, so I leave my hand at my side and look around. The inside of the home is unfinished and mostly a large open space. In the corner is a curtain divider that blocks off a ten foot section of the room. I follow Monroe to the curtain. He pulls it back and there are three women sitting on cots. They don't look up. All are wearing jeans and T-shirts with athletic shoes. I know Monroe provided the clothing. No telling what they were wearing, if anything, when Monroe got to them. The young woman close to me is noticeably shaking. "Do they speak English?" I ask Monroe.

He shakes his head and speaks to the women in Farsi... I think. They scramble off the cots immediately. Monroe introduces us. The woman shaking earlier begins crying. I've been through this many times and the rage builds inside me. The last thing I'll do is show these women how I truly feel, so I smile reassuringly. They get into the car with no hesitation when Monroe walks them outside and points to the vehicle.

"I lost one," Monroe says before I join the driver in the front of the vehicle. Monroe means there were four women and one died. I clench my fists. "I'm sorry," is all I say. His haunted eyes will stay with me. I don't know how he does this but I'm damn glad someone does. These women now have a chance. With a final nod, the car rolls away.

We ride to the airport in silence. I learned a long time ago to say little and get the women to my mother as quickly as possible. There is no language barrier when they finally make it to Mom's. With food, care, and love, she'll bring them around and prove to them that they're no longer in danger.

I fell into my current role as rescuer of human sex slaves purely through my club connection with Monroe. He works for the government but also works outside the law, which makes absolutely no sense. I ask few questions. The women are trained to please men. The training itself is harsh and often deadly when they don't conform. Monroe knows, as I do, that putting these women in a normal environment won't work. They are ill-prepared for the world outside of the sex trade industry they've been rescued from. In many cases, they were sold by their own families and have no place to go. I will finance their new lives and my mom will help them assimilate into our society or she will help them get home if they prefer.

Once we reach the airport's private terminal, the pilot and I situate them for the flight to my mom's home. They say nothing during the entire trip even with headsets. They don't trust me and there's nothing I can do to relieve their fears.

My mother's home rests on two hundred and fifty acres, sixty miles outside the city. She has language specialists, psychologists, and nurses on standby. Monroe will have had them examined by a physician before he turned them over to me. If a medical doctor is needed, we'll provide one. My mom found that not poking and prodding them in the first weeks is best. She hasn't been wrong yet.

Mom greets us as soon as the helicopter lands. She's wearing one of her ever-present gauzy dresses with layers of material and bangles that jingle when she walks. She has no hesitation in welcoming the women with hugs and smiles. They noticeably relax in her presence.

I place a kiss on her cheek when the short greetings are over. "I can't stay," I tell her.

"Of course you can't. My future daughter-in-law needs you." She waves her hand to the helicopter. "Hurry on and seal the deal. I want to meet her."

I probably shouldn't have mentioned Lydia last night. If I don't seal the deal, I'll never hear the end of it. Lydia doesn't know this but she's much better off dealing with me than my mom.

I sleep on the flight back to the hotel and dream of a certain Domme sucking my cock.

Chapter Fifteen

Lydia

I don't see Mr. Lush Lips the next day but he escorts me to the club that night. He says a few clipped sentences and doesn't invite conversation. What a grouch. From the looks of his slightly red eyes, a sleepy grouch. I shouldn't feel sorry for the jerk but I slept like a baby and have a little room to be magnanimous. His damn ass in tight pants helps too.

We part company at the lounge inside the club. I order a strawberry daiquiri. Yep, a girlie drink but I don't care. I never get drunk when I work. Right now I just need a little kick to get Damian's sour mood out of my mind.

I work with two subs without taking pleasure for myself. They don't complain because they leave with red ass cheeks and several orgasms. Angela flits around the club and tells me she's doing great when we have a chance to chat. She needed this. There's no way I would have wanted her working for Johnny Ford. It was hard enough keeping him away from her when she paid his membership fees. She's safe here and accepted. I actually hope she stays after I leave. The environment here is perfect for her.

I don't want to like Damian's club. I need to use this time to gather ideas on how to run my own club. Before Damian, my business plan was based on what not to do. That was easy because if Johnny Ford did it one way, I planned to do the exact opposite. Club El

Diablo, on the other hand, has strict guidelines. Clean bills of health for the clients and a zero tolerance policy when it comes to how subs are treated. The private rooms are monitored, and the entire time I'm in the club I feel safe. At the Mediterranean that was never the case. I worked there in constant fear of the police or that someone would come unhinged and hurt members. I shiver at a memory of an angry customer who almost strangled a sub to death. How Johnny kept the incident quiet is still beyond me. I know large amounts of money had to be involved.

I glance around and my gaze is drawn to the carousel. Damian built a sexual playground for the rich and famous. I never thought I could fit in and only forty-eight hours after arriving, I know I do. I like all the people I've met so far and must remind myself not to become attached. It's one of my many faults and I'll be reminding myself all month.

I have the next two nights off and don't work until Saturday evening. Shopping with Anna and Raul is a blast. Always take a gay man shopping is my motto. He and Anna hit it off and they make plans for her to use him in one of her scenes.

"I don't quite understand why you won't use Raul as your sub," she says when Raul takes a side trip to the men's room. We're at a small pub drinking iced tea.

"It just doesn't feel right," I try to explain. "I wasn't what he needed even though convincing him of that wasn't easy. Raul needs a steady, male Dom who turns him on and won't let him get away with his bratty crap. Watch it or he'll be topping you."

She laughs. "I have a trick or two for naughty subs."

We both laugh. "So give me the lowdown on you and Master D."

Her curiosity is obviously eating her up. "There is no lowdown," I say truthfully. "I want him, he wants me, but we're not playing. Two Doms don't make a right."

She chuckles at my play on words. "He was intense last night, almost volatile when he enacted his scene. He wants you bad and I've never seen him go after a Domme. There isn't a sub at El Diablo that doesn't want his collar." She gives me a level look before going on. "Every so often he'll contract with a sub. Those never last for more than a few months. Believe me it's not due to the subs wanting out. They fall in love with him. Hell, if I were sub material I'd fall in love with him." She shrugs. "Master D is known for losing interest quickly." She scrutinizes me slowly. "That said, he's behaving strangely. Everyone sees it and the tension between the two of you is so thick it's almost a physical presence."

I really don't want to hear any more. I'm already in deep and I need to focus on the end game—my own club. "I'm here for three and a half more weeks. I just can't picture Damian with stripes across his ass. If he wants me, that's what it'll take and we both know that won't happen."

"Oh, girlfriend, truer words have never been spoken." Thankfully she changes the subject. "What brought you into the scene?"

I take a relieved breath. I really don't want to talk about Damian. "When I was eighteen, I fell for an older man. He was a Dom and we spent a very eye-opening weekend together. I wasn't a very good sub and I learned that I wanted to be in charge." I take a sip of iced tea before continuing. "I was quite chubby back then and embarrassed about my body. I began working out, jogging, and then I ordered a bullwhip online. I disposed of most of my apartment furniture, watched videos, and practiced for hours each day. I worked as a secretary during the day but little by little I began exploring the lifestyle at night." I momentarily look away. I've left out so much—hurt and pain really go hand in hand with this story. I only shared those memories with Raul and Sam. "I'm good with a bullwhip and it was great practice for the short whip, which I now prefer."

Anna doesn't pry past what I voluntarily tell her. I ask her the same question and we finish the rest of the conversation with Raul in attendance. He's very good at turning his submissive personality on and off when needed. I know he's lonely for that special someone and has been for a long time. He and Anna will have fun and for now it will do. It's selfish but I don't want him finding that special someone here. I need him for my club. It's our dream.

All in all the shopping trip is a success. I enjoy my days off, spend time with Sam at the park, and watch television with Raul in my suite. I catch his inquisitive looks about every five minutes.

"What?" I finally demand.

"You want him."

I put my hand up. "Stop. I can live without getting what I *want*. Damian is not a man you can easily walk away from. Keeping this a business arrangement is in our club's best interest." Raul smirks and we go back to a really bad B movie that's so bad we laugh through most of it.

I don't see Damian at all during my time off. Saturday arrives and I'm looking forward to working with Angela. Yesterday, I gave Raul a list of what I needed for a new scene I have planned. I gave Angela instructions not to shave or wax intimately before our session.

When it's time for work, I open my door after a light knock expecting Damian. He sent Carl to do the honors of escorting me to the club via a private elevator. I refuse to ask Carl about Mr. Succulent Semen.

The smell of sex and leather instantly hits me when we enter, taking me fully into my Domme zone. My scene is set up as I requested. This is a role-play session because I want to have some fun. "Do you trust me?"

"Yes, Mistress."

"Okay, remember your safe word. I won't take you further than you can go but tonight I'm pushing." I kiss her forehead and love the lovely tremble of her lips.

I point down to the carpet. "Disrobe and take your position." Angela removes her short dress, folds it, and puts it to the side. She drops to her knees with her legs slightly open and her palms facing up on her thighs.

A crowd forms around us. I get it, I'm new. I also have a reputation to uphold. When I'm ready, I place her on the St. Andrew's Cross facing me. Using an expensive shaving gel that Raul spent too much money on and a sharp razor, I shave her pussy with slow, steady strokes. I slip one hand between the wood of the cross and her ass and massage her rounded bottom. She squirms and receives a smart slap to her leg. "Steady," I tell her and smile to the side where she can't see me. Her cunt is begging for my fingers but I have no intention of giving it what it needs right away. I trail a finger between her ass cheeks and still don't touch her where she really needs it.

She groans.

"Shh, no sounds, we've only just started," I whisper.

"Ahhh, please, Mistress."

I shake my head. Angela's already become spoiled at Damian's club. "Angela, my sweet sub, your punishment will be the delay of your orgasm." I planned to give the crowd a good show and now I'll withhold her first release as part of that show.

I start with a deerskin flogger and concentrate on her breasts and upper thighs. I avoid her freshly shaved pussy knowing it's begging for pain and pleasure.

She whimpers. I have no mercy. I'm not using vaginal or anal toys. I want her writhing from the feel of the soft leather strands striking her body. After several stinging strikes, I stop for a moment and lean in close to Angela. I take one tight nipple into my mouth, suck hard, and then move to the other nipple when her legs stiffen within the bindings. I'm being especially cruel tonight and giving her just enough to drive her crazy.

I use the flogger again until she moans loudly. It's now time for the blindfold. I add a quick kiss on her lips to calm her once she's blind to what's about to happen. As prearranged, Kyle approaches the cross and disrobes. He massages his burgeoning erection until it's at full mast. He slides a condom over himself when I nod.

Kyle prefers giving pain. I'm fully aware that the level of pain Kyle works with is extreme. I'm not entirely sure why he agreed to help me with Angela. I adjust the cross so Angela is lying on her back. Kyle straddles her hips. I squeeze between Kyle and Angela's upper body. With the blindfold, she can't see what we we're doing or who's doing what. My heels are barely touching the carpet but I manage to lean down and take a nipple between my lips. I add teeth and bite hard enough that her pelvis lifts from the bench. Kyle plunges inside her offered pussy in one smooth thrust.

Angela screams, Kyle moans, and I watch as Angela jerks against the restraints. My pussy clenches and I wonder how long I'll be able to resist Damian. A shiver passes over my skin and the air changes subtly. I open my eyes and Damian's standing a few feet away. He's massaging his cock with a steamy look in his eyes. He's wearing a pair of sexy black jeans that leave nothing to the imagination. He sees me watching him and ever so slowly, he unzips himself and pulls his cock free. I watch in lustful fascination as he strokes his hand up and down his incredible length. He doesn't bother looking at the sub kneeling at his side. He threads his fingers into her hair and pulls her close to his cock until her lips open and he thrusts in. The entire time he stares at me. I need an ice cold shower for me and a baseball bat to knock out the little sub's teeth.

Kyle's hands go to my hips as he changes his angle on Angela. His gripping fingers snap me out of my less-than-pleasant thoughts. I owe my sub and the crowd a few more orgasms. It's time for the first toy of the evening.

Damian's fingers grip the sub's hair tighter and I know exactly when he loses it. For several seconds he closes his eyes. I watch the tightening of his jaw and the slight parting of his lips. The sub is talented and she takes him almost completely down her throat as he orgasms.

His eyes open and burn into mine. We both want the same fucking thing and I'm using everything at my disposal to stop myself from giving in. Damian helps his sub to her feet and steers her away from my area. I breathe a sigh of relief when he's finally out of sight. Kyle pinches my hip and lets me know he's fully aware that I'm momentarily not mentally present in the scene. Bad Domme. I pull my thoughts away from Mr. Gargantuan Dick and give the crowd and Angela what they came for. Angela cries beautiful tears when I finally allow her relief from the stimulation we're forcing on her. She's so beautiful when she orgasms and a round of applause ends the scene.

Angela's exhausted by the time she's moved to the post-scene area. I take extra time with her aftercare so she knows how much I appreciate her trust. Using another Dom or Domme was never going to happen at the MC and I felt bad. There was no one I trusted enough with her fragile state. It says a lot that I trust Kyle after just meeting him. Maybe it's his haunted eyes.

"I like it here, Mistress," Angela tells me once she's back in control.

I do too but I don't say that. "When it's time for me to leave, you can stay. I'll work something out with Master D for your dues."

Her eyes flash to mine and tears slowly start forming. "I need you, Mistress."

It's sad because really we need each other. She's such a damaged soul and she feeds the damage I carry inside myself. I won't encourage her to come with me when Raul and I leave. I'll do my damnedest to find her a Dom or Domme who will take care of her. I'll fucking miss her, though, and it sucks.

When Angela is calm and rested, Anna walks over and invites me to a private party in one of the suites after work. I leave the club at two in the morning and head back to my room to change. I let Samson out, give him a snack because I'm leaving him again, and go search for the party. Anna told me it wasn't a D/s party and that's why I changed. This is a good, old-fashioned, let's get drunk and celebrate Saturday night party. Or more precisely, celebrate early Sunday morning party. I'm wearing what Damian refers to as my hippie clothes. He had my closet stocked full of them. The thought actually makes me smile. I can't fault him for his well thought out details that make life a breeze for me.

Thirty minutes later, I'm tipsy and taking a sip of my third margarita when the devil walks through the door wearing his customary dark clothing. He's a beacon in a room full of dazzling people and it's nearly impossible to slide my gaze away. He's so fucking hot. Too hot for me to handle. Instead of watching Damian, I drag my attention to one of the male Club El Diablo bartenders and do something I never do. I flirt.

A few minutes later, steel fingers press into my shoulders and hot breath passes over my bare neck before traveling to my ear. "I want you." I know it's him by smell and touch alone. The ever-present pussy zing I get whenever he's close goes into high mode and I clench my thighs together for a few seconds. Turning in the stool, I place my thighs on the outside of his hips. My skirt pulls tight but Damian doesn't let that stop him. He lifts the skirt up past my knees so he can slide in closer. My lips shy down his neck but I don't touch until I gently bite his earlobe. In the breathiest whisper I can manage, I reply, "No."

His hands slide under my bottom and he positions the center of my thighs to his hard erection. His mouth goes back to my ear. "I have a wager for you," he whispers so low a thrill runs through me at his tone more than his words.

Our voices are low but I'm sure everyone in the room is watching our sexual play. "Terms?"

He bites my earlobe like I did his a few seconds ago. "Two subs." He licks down the bend of my ear and I inhale sharply. "Blindfolds. Whips only." His hands squeeze my thighs with his fingers so close to my pussy I swear I can already feel them there. "No toys," he continues. "They won't know who's working who. First one to bring their sub to orgasm wins."

Fuck me but I'm so in. "What's the payout?"

Now his hands go feather soft across my skin. "One night as the other's personal sub."

I pull back and look into his shadowed, sensual eyes. I'm beyond tipsy and have no control over what spills from my mouth. "You would sub for me?" I breathe on a sigh at the image that clicks into my brain.

Pure wickedness sparkles in his eyes. "I have no intention of losing, Lydia."

Holly S. Roberts

Chapter Sixteen

Damian

I staked my claim last night. Gossip is ramped at the best of times at the club. Now it's wildfire. I made my move because I wanted everyone to know, especially the men, that Lydia is off limits. I didn't like her working a scene with Kyle and I didn't like her flirting with the bartender. My brain tells me how wrong I am to expect submission from a Domme, but my dick feels the intensity of her stare. Lydia wants me, but she's too stubborn to act on it.

I'm tired of waiting.

After stacking the deck on my first bet with the lovely Lydia, this second one could go either way. I haven't felt this level of exhilaration in ages. I *will* win this bet.

Of course, the day of the bet is spent dealing with a million and one petty items within the hotel. I have an excellent hotel manager, but it just so happens he's on vacation and I'm stuck doing the everyday tasks I've never enjoyed. A fight broke out in housekeeping. Not a yelling match, an all-out brawl between two women. Both were fired on the spot. It's times like this that I wish the entire world was made up of dominants and submissives. It would be so much easier to punish them with an aggressive paddling than to sign their separation papers. After a brief meeting with their supervisor, I'm given no choice. Their bickering has impeded the work of other employees.

Ten minutes after security escorts the women off the premises, there's another crisis in the main restaurant kitchen. I decide right then that I'm promoting an assistant manager to co-manage the El Diablo Hotel. I'm not doing this again. Call me spoiled but why amass a fortune if you can't hire good people to take some of the load off your back.

It's after three in the afternoon when I find time to take a break and call my mother.

"They're doing well," she says immediately after answering. "One is having more trouble than the other two but I've seen worse. They are cooking tonight's dinner and like the other girls that have come through here, they want to stay busy. Donya, you remember her, don't you?"

The name rings a small bell. She's one of the women my mom worked with last year. I give an affirmative response.

"She speaks Farsi and she's moving in and helping us with the language barrier. The women aren't saying much yet but that's okay. They have time." My mom loves what she does. She's a mother through and through. She stops talking and remains silent for about twenty seconds. "Well?" she finally asks.

"I'm working on it. We have a bet that I plan on winning."

Mom laughs. "Do I want to know what the bet is?"

"No, you don't."

Her laughter is louder now. "I love that a woman is finally getting to you. It's about time."

"I don't like it," I say like a spoiled child.

"Of course you don't but nothing worth having comes easy. The more she pushes your buttons the more you'll want her and that's a good thing."

All the shit my mom put up with regarding my father made her a stronger woman. "I'll call and give you an update after I win."

"I hope you don't mind that I'm cheering for her. Even if you lose, I have faith you'll find a way past her shields."

We end the call and I punch in Monroe's number to give him an update. He says little and ends the call without so much as a goodbye. That's Monroe. The man is king at working in the background, saving the weak, and handing out punishment to those who break the law. I have no doubt the men responsible don't survive Monroe's wrath. In my opinion, if he decides someone needs to disappear, it needs to be permanent. My office phone buzzes, and after swearing under my breath, I head to the next disaster.

Chapter Seventeen

Lydia

Our bet makes the club grapevine heat up. We arrange the whip-off for Monday, usually the slowest night at the club. The place is packed and even more crowded than it was Saturday night.

I should have known.

Damian picks the subs. They're friends, both female, and they enjoy working together and partnering with one Dom. The rules make them smile and I have no doubt they'll be the most popular subs in the club during the next week. Neither one will know who wields their whip. No broken skin or the bet is forfeit. First sub to orgasm wins the contest for their dominant.

Damian had another St. Andrew's Cross moved into the largest station area where we're prepping. We blindfold the naked women and then Damian gives me dibs on the sub I want. I take the blonde. She's moving around on her toes in anticipation and from the way I see it, she'll orgasm quickly.

I spent the day thinking about ways Damian could cheat. He's given me first choice, which moves the bet into my favor. I know him, though, and I wouldn't put anything past him. I just don't have a clue what that *anything* is.

My hand trembles slightly while I rotate my wrist. I inhale deeply to steady my nerves. *I will win this*, I tell myself silently. It becomes a litany. We are working with six-foot whips. I'm good with one but prefer my four-footer. It takes a lot of space to wield a whip this length. Damian has everyone step back so we have room to work without worrying about what's behind us. I refuse to watch Damian prepare and I stay focused on my warmup. Managing my heartrate is another story. It's thumping so hard I'm surprised the people fifteen feet away can't hear it.

I might not be watching Damian warm up but my body knows he's there. It's like I have butterfly wings lightly floating across my skin. Just his scent sends energy ricocheting straight to my pussy. It's completely unfair that he has this effect on me. I catch just the sight of him from the corner of my eye and the damn man has removed his shirt. I turn my head and take a quick glimpse because I can't help myself.

A light trail of hair slides down past the waist of his leather pants and I want to follow the path it takes under the leather and even further down. He's killing me. Movement to my other side gains my attention and I slowly pull my gaze away from Damian. Raul covertly rolls his eyes because he noticed where my gaze was. If I wasn't the center of attention, I'd stick my tongue out.

At the loud snap of Damian's whip, I return my focus to him. He nods with a Cheshire cat smile and I nod back. The wager begins.

I would normally approach the sub first, but I can't give away who I am. Out of habit, I check around me, place the wrist loop around my wrist, grip the handle firmly, and bring the whip up circling it over my head. The first snap is almost simultaneous with Damian's.

I inhale and exhale slowly while concentrating on the task at hand—getting my sweet little sub off. I work her slow with little pain and allow her to become accustomed to the feel of the fall going around her arms and legs. I know from personal experience that what

I'm doing is erotic. The leather whispers around the areas I strike in gentle swirls. Every four or five lashes, I wrap the whip around her chest allowing the popper to tickle her breasts. Slowly, I increase the force of the leather thong hitting her thighs. With no warning, I snap the whip so the popper hits her pussy. The response is instant and I back off slightly in my intensity. And it all starts over again. With no other stimulation, this isn't an easy task. My focus remains entirely on my sub and her pending release.

It takes about twenty minutes and she's so damn close I can taste it. I cast my first glance at Damian. He's not working his whip—he's staring at me. My gaze goes to his sub. She hangs limp in her restraints.

With purposeful strides, Damian walks over, removes the whip from my hand, and passes it to another Dom. I don't even see who it is. I'm transfixed by the devil's gaze. I'm hot, sweaty, and terrified all at once. And, I'm also so fucking turned on, it's hard to breathe.

He won.

As it sinks in, I look around for an escape route, which is stupid but I do it anyway. His warm body leans into mine and my world tilts when Damian hoists me over his shoulder. A round of applause breaks out. My damn ass is on display for everyone.

I lost. Fuck.

The blinking lights go by as Damian carries me through the club straight to his back office. He stops only long enough to punch in the access code for his private elevator.

"You can put me down now, I'm not going anywhere," I say with my cheek resting against his backside.

A heavy slap lands on my ass.

"You don't have permission to speak. You know the rules."

Another hard slap lands for emphasis, but besides my quick inhale, I remain quiet. I won't deny I want this. My desire is at a fever pitch. It sucks that I don't want him to know how I feel. What would it be like to let go, give Damian the lead, and enjoy what's about to happen? I can't, I remind myself silently. I need to keep my focus on the end game, which is owning my own club. He carries me into the elevator and my stomach tightens as we travel upward. All I can see is Damian's delectable backside and the plush black carpeting.

He steps off the elevator into the penthouse. I try to take in the surroundings but I'm upended again and my butt hits a hard wooden chair. He leaves me there and walks away while I gape.

I expected opulence and it's exactly what I get. Every detail of the room screams money. The artwork alone is breathtaking. Damian walks over to me carrying a yellow folder, two wine glasses, and a bottle... Borgogno. I know it's expensive; why would I expect anything less?

I keep my mouth closed like a good little sub, giving him no reason to discipline me again. For one night, I can play his game. He will never know I crave so much more.

His eyebrow arches. Apparently, he's expecting a comment. I look down at my interlocked fingers resting in my lap. He wanted it. He got it.

He tilts my chin up with one finger and our eyes meet.

"If you keep a civil tongue, you may speak. Your insolent mouth will only get you punished, so be careful." He releases me and pours two glasses of wine.

I look at the glass he holds out. "You know it's not a good idea to drink in this situation and I'd rather keep my wits about me."

"You need to relax. One glass of wine will help with that. We're going through your soft and hard limits and then you're signing the agreement."

"The deal was carte blanche. Why do you care what my limits are?" I seriously can't help my Domme voice when I say it.

He lets my snippy tone go without reprimand. "Good question, but I'm not a complete sadist and I'd like you to get something out of this evening. This is not up for discussion—the wine or the contract. If you come away with bruises, I don't want the cops at my door."

Embarrassingly enough, my hand shakes when I take the glass from his hand. Damian's eyes miss nothing but he doesn't comment. He opens the folder and takes out the contract. It's the same one used in the club. Heat rushes into my face, which causes Damian's dimples to show, damn him.

"Do you wish to go through this one by one or would you rather just tell me what I need to know?" He rests the contract in front of me. "You need to understand that I will counter your demands with some of my own and we'll compromise on a few items. Both our needs are being met tonight."

I want to scream at the ridiculousness of what's about to go down. Instead, I give my first hard limit. "Anal sex is off the table."

He doesn't blink. "Okay. I can work with that, but I will use anal toys."

"It's the same thing." Yes, my whiny voice betrays me.

He shakes his head. "No, it isn't. My cock up your ass is anal sex. The toys are anal play. There's a huge difference." Huge as in the size of his cock, but he doesn't say it. He checks the box for anal sex as a hard limit. "Next item."

I swallow the rest of my wine in one unladylike gulp. I hope it costs thousands of dollars.

Damian bites his lip, fighting his goddamn smile. This night is never going to end.

We go through it all—no animals, no wet play, no fire play. He gets hot wax. Ouch. He promises no blisters if he uses wax. It takes almost an hour. By the end of our discussion, I know I'm in deep trouble.

"I'll show you to the bathroom. I want you showered, your hair washed, body shaved, and ready in twenty minutes. Everything you need is on the counter in the bathroom. There's a robe on the back of the door and you will come out with the robe untied. Don't comb your hair, only wrap it in a towel. When you approach me, you will kneel at my feet facing me in the proper position. Is there anything you're unclear about?"

"No," I grumble.

His lips press firmly together and it doesn't take a rocket scientist to I know I crossed a line. "No, Sir," I amend.

He stands and leads me through his bedroom to the bathroom. It's magnificent—gray marble with black accents. He leaves the door open a crack and walks away. I look at the door and think about closing it. Hell. It's not worth the fight.

I pee first and even his damn toilet paper is luxurious. The oversized shower has two showerheads, water jets above and to the sides, and bench seats on both sides. I could truly live in here for a full week. I unplait my braid and lather my hair quickly, remembering his time limit. My cunt, legs, and arms are silky smooth when I finish shaving. I can't help myself and run my fingers through my hair to get out a few of the tangles.

My time is up and there's no sense postponing the inevitable.

Damian is standing by the bed when I come out. He's changed into a pair of black cotton pants and his delectable chest remains bare along with his feet. I go to my knees while trying to control my breathing.

"Spread your knees farther," he barks.

I obey.

Damian gently unwraps the towel from my hair and tosses it on the floor beside me. The wet strands cascade in front of my eyes, obscuring my face. His body folds in front of me and I can see his smooth chest through the strands. He begins running a comb through the tangles. No tugging or pulling. He meticulously takes his time.

My pussy grows damp.

It's too much.

I realize what this night will mean. Tears well in my eyes. Damian tilts my chin up. I keep my eyes down and don't meet his. His warm breath hits my cheek a second before his tongue flicks out and collects the tears.

"None of that," he whispers. "Tonight is about pleasure. Forget our lives, the club, and if you can, your objections. I won't take more than you give."

"Bu…"

His finger covers my lips. "You no longer have permission to speak." The words are breathy soft in my ear. He places soft kisses on my hairline, the corner of my eye, and then moves to my lips. The kiss is sensual and loving. This is not what I expected from Damian. I unclench my fingers and move them to my thighs digging my fingers into my skin. It takes everything I have to resist running my fingers through his hair. He smells so damn good.

He pulls away. "Tell me something about yourself that my investigators couldn't uncover. Something private," he whispers.

I don't hesitate. "No."

He pushes a lock of hair behind my ear. "That's your favorite word. You don't play the submissive very well." There's a light tone in his voice like he's teasing me.

"I'm not a sub," I answer in my defense. Oh, but I am in the bedroom and he thankfully doesn't know that.

"Tonight you are," he says in his dominant voice that leaves no room for argument.

I remain silent while staring into his eyes. Does he read me this easily? I do everything I can to keep my expression blank.

He grins and his face goes from handsome to breathtaking. "Another wager?" he asks.

His beautiful smile throws me and I stumble over my words. "Not a, ah, good idea." I add an eye roll so he doesn't catch on that I'm in lust with him and his stunning dimples.

His, "Tsk, tsk," almost makes me smile.

Even knowing wagers have caused all my current problems I can't help myself. "Five orgasms?"

No hesitation whatsoever. "Yours or mine?" he asks.

I finally smile. "Mine."

"And your forfeit when you lose?"

I don't miss the cockiness of his question. "I won't lose. A week of submission."

"Then we've reached a deal."

I expect him to shake my hand but instead his fingers brush aside the bathrobe and he covers my breasts with his palms. "I knew these were soft, but they're actually pure silk. They fit my hands so perfectly." His thumbs and forefingers not so gently pinch my nipples, sending a jolt straight to my pussy. "These first." He pinches my nipples again. "It's time we get started. Eyes down."

He stands and walks away. My eyes are down but I can see him as he strolls around. God, even his bare feet turn me on. He returns and kneels in front of me again. His hand opens and nipple clamps rest on his palm. These are pinch-y but don't have teeth. I would have used the more painful ones on him because I'm mean that way. He leans forward and takes one aching nipple into his warm mouth. My toes curl. He sucks and flicks the delicate flesh. It's impossibly hard not to moan. Giving him that advantage this early is not in my plans. He pulls away slowly, his eyes glued to my wet nipple. He attaches the first clamp. I inhale sharply. There may be no teeth but he slides the pressure flange high up the clamp to make sure I feel it.

"You have a safe word. I expect you to know your limits while teaching me what your body needs."

He doesn't wait for my reply, just begins working on the other nipple. When he's finished, a small chain runs between my breasts. It has very small bells that jingle slightly when he plumps my breasts. I know he's smiling but I don't look up. With the clamps on my nipples and his dimples showing, I might orgasm on the spot. *Bad sub*, I silently admonish myself.

Damian stands and moves behind me. His fingers run through my hair and then he divides it into three sections and deftly braids it down the back. After securing it with an unseen hair tie, he places his hands on my shoulders.

"Come," he whispers in my ear sending shivers down my spine. He releases me and walks from the room. He has no idea that I almost had my first orgasm because of his words alone. I'll come all right but I can guaran-damn-tee it won't be five times.

Chapter Eighteen

Damian

Feeling her hair between my fingers is almost better than sucking her amazing breasts. Almost. Her skin is so damn smooth. Absolute perfection. But this hair. I want to wrap it around my cock while she sucks me dry. I can do basic rope work but to do what I really want with her hair, I need a few added lessons. I'll hit up Monroe for instruction the next time he visits the club.

Tonight is about offering pleasure and giving my lady five orgasms. Lydia thinks she can withstand what's about to happen. I know differently. When I touch her shoulders, goose bumps run across her skin. The longer she's on her knees, the more shallow her breathing becomes. I'm sure she doesn't even realize the many delectable signals her body gives off.

And oh, what a body. She's poetry with all the right curves in the perfect places. A bit too thin maybe, but she has a large build, which to me is the picture of perfection.

The truth is she has no idea what I'm willing to do for her. If she called a stop right now, I would drop to my knees and submit. I've never felt this way about a woman. Her dominance turns me on and, at the same time, complements my own. All these years I've been searching for that special sub. Now I realize I never found her because it's not what I actually need. Lydia challenges me and I find that the biggest turn on of all.

Crazy.

It's hard to take my hands from her shoulders because I want to push her forward and sink my cock deep inside her pussy. I'm stronger than that, though.

It's time to play.

Chapter Nineteen

Lydia

I follow Damian when he beckons and keep my eyes down as much as possible. I know my role. I'm not sure how many rooms we pass as we walk through a large section of the penthouse until he opens a door and nods for me to precede him down a flight of stairs. There are eight. I watch my feet and count each one. The smell of leather enters my nostrils and grows stronger with each step.

I stop at the bottom knowing that by the little I can see we're in Damian's private dungeon. My knees almost give out as anticipation rolls through me.

His warm hands startle me when they land on my upper arms, his fingers clenching my skin just tight enough to show who's in charge. I feel his hot breath right before he places a feather-soft kiss on my bare neck. He takes my hand and leads me across the room to a long, narrow table with a bar overhead. He steps behind me and slips the bathrobe completely off my shoulders. It pools at my feet with a slight whoosh of air.

He turns me around so I'm facing him. I don't look up as he takes in the sight of me completely naked. He says nothing, and a minute later, his hands go to the backs of my thighs.

"Hold onto my neck," he orders.

He lifts me to the edge of the table. His large body moves between my closed legs, pushing my knees apart.

He backs away. "Don't move."

He says nothing about my coming orgasm and I really need one. Right. Fucking. Now. Instead, he walks over to a cabinet against a side wall and removes several items before returning. He places something behind my back on the bench and then takes my right wrist and places a leather cuff around it. It's the Velcro type, about two inches wide with soft lamb's wool on the underside. A thrill shoots through me when he tightens the first one.

The men I invite into my bedroom will pull my hair and boss me around. They are not true dominants and can barely call themselves a top. Damian breathes dominance and he knows all the little ways to increase the tension of a scene. The California kink community is close knit. I earned my living as an edgy Domme who's good with a whip. Publically seeking out a dominant to get me off wasn't something I was willing to risk. My mystique was half the allure and I needed every lousy dime Johnny Ford paid me.

Damian repeats the process with my other wrist and the momentary haze in my brain subsides. He takes both my arms and clips them to the bar above my head. My pussy throbs, my nipples continue to burn, and it's all I can do not to insist he immediately fuck me.

"This will allow you to hold the bar," he breathes against my arm. At this point, my skin is extra sensitive and just that breath of air nearly sends me over the edge. Each whisper of breath, touch of fingers, and command pull me further under his spell. The idea is for me to win this bet. I must hold myself to four orgasms. Easy.

He moves the bar, which attaches to a sliding mechanism. I move with it and lean back against the table with my arms suspended upward. "I thought we would get this part out of the way," he offers after positioning me for whatever is to come. Hopefully me.

I forget my place as a good sub and turn my head so I can see him. I hadn't realized he'd picked up lube and a medium sized butt plug before he lowered me onto the bench. It's funny, I don't mind anal play when I'm working with a sub. For some reason, it triggers my submissive brain at the thought of Damian's cock in my ass. I need to hide that from him and just try to enjoy what he's planning. Yeah, that doesn't happen. It's pure reflex when he moves his hands to my ass. My legs come up and I kick out.

Damian moves back. "So you want to play?" His eyes tell me how badly I've messed up. Shit. He grabs my legs in a tight grip and removes a larger ankle cuff from his back pocket. Now I really start to fight. A swift stinging slap lands on my hip. It hurts and works its way into my panicked brain. He slaps the same spot again and I stop struggling with a heavy exhale. "You have a safe word. If you behave like that again without using it, you won't enjoy the consequences." Flat. Final. And infuriating.

He spreads my legs wide, bends my knees, and secures my ankles to the table. My butt is barely touching. I try closing my knees, but two inflexible hands hold them apart. Damian is affected by my bratty behavior. I hear it in his voice. He releases one knee and circles my pussy with a finger. I'm so damn wet. I watch his face when he discovers my desire. He's hot as fuck, but in full Dom mode, he's my fantasy. His brown eyes lift to mine and slowly he brings his finger to his lips.

"I've wanted to taste you since the first night." He licks the glistening moisture. "Delicious," he says after licking it clean. His finger returns to my pussy and enters, pushing deeper this time. I gasp.

He slides in slowly and pulls out just as slowly. My hips lift up, raising my ass even more. His other hand splays over my stomach to hold me down. "Don't move," he says with a raspy voice.

I lower my head to the bench while taking deep calming breaths. He removes his finger and I hear him opening the lube and squirting it onto the butt plug. My sphincter muscles tighten. This will be uncomfortable. I'm unaccustomed to anal play. A finger travels between my butt cheeks seeking the hole I want him staying away from. He lubricates the puckered circle without entering. He plays gently with my asshole and unexpectedly his mouth finds the hot folds of my pussy. His tongue flicks against my clit, causing my hips to buck off the table again.

His laugh is low and sexy. "The first thing I thought I would need was a gag for your mouth, but you've been unexpectedly quiet these last minutes." He gives me a devilish grin. "Unfortunately, you can't stay still and I'll need to help you with that." He pulls straps from the sides of the table and secures them firmly over my hips. He doesn't give me time to adjust and his sweet mouth goes back to work. His finger slides into my pussy again and his lips target my clit with a bit of suction.

There's a ball of fire in my belly and it travels from my pussy to my nipples, growing stronger with each passing second. I thrash against the bindings and moan. His mouth continues torturing me and there's nothing I can do but give in. The muscles of my pussy spasm and a sharp cry escapes me as the orgasm rolls throughout my body. I'm riding the waves and barely notice the pressure against my asshole. The plug goes past the tight bundle of nerves and lodges deep in my ass. Pulses continue rolling through me. Damian moves back to my pussy and nibbles my clit. My moan is much louder this time as I ride the waves that have never been this powerful in my life.

The world comes into focus when the orgasm finally tapers off. I open my eyes and he's watching me. A small section of hair has come loose from my braid and he slides it behind my ear. "Your job is simple," he says and I'm amazed he's so calm after my world exploded. "You need to clench the plug tightly. If it falls out, there will be hell to pay, and the next one I use won't be as small."

I fight the high-pitched shriek I want to let loose and scream silently in my head. His eyes aren't softened with passion; the damn things sparkle with mirth. "One down and four to go," he says with more enjoyment than he has a right to.

Three more is all he'll get from me. I will control this. If I weren't restrained and at his mercy, I'd throw something at him.

Holly S. Roberts

Chapter Twenty

Damian

She's unreal and her responsiveness is out of this world. I actually worried that with me in control she wouldn't get off. I get it. We're dominant. I had this nice little checklist for my perfect sub. Before Lydia's orgasm, I couldn't check any of them off my list.

Seeing her come changes everything. I also throw that mental list away. Lydia is just more. More fire. More beautiful. Just more. She fights it and she would bite my head off if I told her she has a hidden submissive running around inside her. What am I thinking? She knows her own damn body.

She knows.

Since seeing her for the first time, I've run so many possibilities through my mind. Asking Lydia about a vanilla relationship was at the top of my list. I was so desperate and willing to give it a try myself if it helped get her out of my system. Now, that's not what I want.

She's a fiery Domme with a submissive streak. Why does she hide it? From what I can tell, she's not a switch. When she plays, she's dominant. This entire situation is tricky at best. I need Lydia to let go. Yes, her last orgasm was spectacular, but it could be so much more.

I know she isn't completely averse to ass play because I've watched her torture subs with it. When she told me no anal I thought she was playing me and being a brat. Her tantrum showed me something different. If I didn't know better, I would think her afraid.

Lydia has so many layers, maybe too many, and I will never understand them all. This last thought travels straight to my cock and it stiffens painfully. Yes. I want to peel back those layers and see what she hides. Discover what makes her tick. And yes, open up to her. I want that connection like I've never wanted it before.

Lydia's mine even if she doesn't know it yet. More than that—I'm hers. I want her to be part of my business and fully integrated in my life. They say we all have another half waiting for us. The instant connection I had with Lydia makes me believe in fate. I'm a practical man and would have told you before that soulmate connections were bullshit. Watching Lydia now, I know it's true. Her green eyes blaze with indignation. It's really sad that I also crave her tears. I want her completely at my mercy physically and mentally. I want her to give in to my domination. I want her begging for my touch, kneeling because it's what she wants, and fucking me. I want nothing about her to change.

She's twisted me into someone I don't recognize.

And the bigger question is… how the hell do I keep her in my life?

Chapter Twenty-One

Lydia

My wrist and ankle cuffs remain after Damian releases me from the table. He also leaves the butt plug and nipple clamps. I know he's aware the clamps can't stay on much longer, but I know better than to point this out. If he doesn't take them off soon, I'll scream to the rafters over what an idiot Dom he is.

He steers me to a spanking bench. Regardless of the evidence of my arousal, I will not lose this bet. It's totally a normal occurrence for the silky wetness from my last orgasm to slide down my legs. Okay, slight exaggeration there. This has never happened.

With a firm push between my shoulder blades, he guides me down so my ass is in the air. Without speaking, he quickly secures my wrists and ankles to the bench. I jump slightly when his finger slides between my ass cheeks and stops at the butt plug. I clench my ass tightly, refusing to release the toy when he gives a slight tug. He's quite insistent on playing with my ass, and a soft groan escapes from deep in my throat.

He's so matter-of-fact when he decides to gift me with his voice. "I know you want my cock in here." He twists the damn thing, causing me to fidget. "But it's too late to go back on the contract now." The muscles of my poor abused asshole ache as he continues twisting, pulling, and pushing the damn thing back in. The pain is bearable, just. It also takes me from plus two on the "needs an orgasm scale" to a plus eight. If he touches my clit, he'll have two orgasms in his favor. He stops, places a warm hand on my shoulder, and my cramped toes relax.

"This is the punishment I've dreamed about giving you since the first night we met." His hand slides down my back to the swell of my hip and he leans in close to my ear. "It's going to hurt and you're going to cry. I promise we'll both love it."

Panic sets in. He's doing this on purpose, and I'll be damned if I cry no matter how bad this is. I watch him closely as he heads to the wall and takes down a black leather riding crop. Yeah, the slight mischievous grin on his face when he carries it back over doesn't help my soured mood. I'm lying lengthwise on the bench with my breasts to either side of the ten-inch wide apparatus and my legs hanging over the end. The first touch of the crop on my tender, clamped nipples makes me inhale sharply. I burn from breasts to pussy and I swear my blood catches fire, causing my breath to grow erratic. I actually press my cunt as hard as possible against the leather. Does it help? Hell no.

He stops and moves behind me, where I can't see him. In a very Dom voice, he startles me. "Do you remember the first night we met?" Without giving me a chance to reply, the crop comes down hard across my right ass cheek. The slight squeal that escapes my mouth pisses me off. I inhale, count to three, and then exhale. I can take this.

"I expect an answer." The crop lands again in the exact spot as the last strike. I hold back a groan.

"Yes," I reply between clenched teeth. "I remember."

This time the crop slides across the flesh of my left cheek. "Did you really think I would hurt you?" The crop lands again. The pain is more intense because he strikes the same spot twice.

"I didn't know you," I manage to say after I exhale.

"You're so beautiful, a witch in disguise." The next strike lands on the tender skin right beneath my butt cheek. "You sent me flying over your shoulder." The second strike, the same. This is all a prelude to ten strikes in a row shared between the tender skin on the back of my leg and my ass cheeks. I'm barely holding it together when he speaks again. "I wanted to strangle you, but more than anything, I wanted to fuck you." The crop lands on my exposed pussy and the scream I've been holding back rips from my throat.

Okay, I can accept that I won't get out of this without some unpleasant sounds. It's the tears I fight. I can handle all the pain he dishes out. Then his palm smooths over my back and he comforts me as I try to gain control of my breathing. It's his gentleness that breaks something. My tears start flowing just like he said they would.

His other hand glides across my skin, over my hip, and between my legs. Ever so slowly, two fingers enter me as far as they'll go. I'm filled with Damian Collins. I wiggle to take more until he twists the butt plug. "Damn you," I cry out while doing everything I can to hold back another orgasm. I'm on the ledge, tipping over head first. I bite down on my tongue to stop the coming tide. Not because I don't want the orgasm, but because I hate that he controls it so easily. Between my tears and the need for him to fuck me, I'm putty in his hands and I don't like it. I don't want him reducing me to a slobbering mess, because I'm a big bad Domme and I don't show emotion like this. Or at least I never have before.

Damian's warm breath hits the side of my neck. "Oh, baby, you're playing right into my hands." He goes back to work with the crop, using extra force. I don't have time to scream before the next strike lands. He systematically turns me into a giant ball of need. His aim is perfect and now, he's decided not to hit the same place twice.

My ass and thighs are a wash of fire. He finishes this torture with another lash to my pussy. His fingers take over, the butt plug twists, and my resolve weakens. Hell, it disappears entirely.

The explosion rips through me in endless waves of pleasure. My body fires on all circuits. My nerve endings fry, my brain goes haywire, and my cunt pulses to some unheard music.

Low light finally invades my vision. I have no idea how much time has passed. That was the best damn orgasm I've had in my entire life.

Damian releases my arms and adjusts the bench downward before assisting me off. I sink to my knees with his slight nudge to my sweaty shoulder. When I'm able to, I glance up and see that Damian's in front of me gazing down. He calls me beautiful, but really it's he who holds the title. His fierce look of pure dominant pride makes me want to kiss his feet. "Unzip my pants and take my cock into your mouth. Use your hands on my balls. I like a small amount of pain, so keep that in mind. You will drink me down and lick my cock clean." It's a command, and who am I to deny a Master?

With shaking hands, I manage his zipper. He's commando and it's near impossible to get the material to give enough. His large cock springs free when I've all but given up. I push the clinging material slightly past his hips so I can palm his balls. I squeeze just enough. If nothing else, I'm good at judging what men need to orgasm as quickly as possible or delay it for hours. Damian's fingers sink into my braid. His cock is gorgeous—long, thick, and oh so lickable. His cock is an extension of his dominance. I tighten my hold on his balls and take his bobbing dick with the other hand and my lips slip around him. I create a swirling motion with my tongue just at the head. He's impatient with my teasing and pushes my head forward, forcing me to take several inches into my mouth.

The sexy timbre of his voice echoes slightly in the room and sends shivers across my flesh. "I've dreamed of this. Your mouth is so damn hot. Suck me, baby. Use your teeth." I glance up and his head is back, his long throat tense. I think Damian enjoys pain as much as I do, and something inside me twists. Unfortunately, I don't have time to put all the little boxes in their correct departments because the cock in my mouth needs what I have to give. I pull back and nibble and then lick. Damian groans low in his throat and I add more teeth. He's mine. I increase the assault on his cock and his breath turns ragged just like mine was minutes ago. I love the dominance of a blow job, and sucking off Damian is pure pleasure. I specialize in men who enjoy pain. If only I could tie his hands and make this last for hours. Yes, hours. I'm that evil.

The hot spill of semen fills my mouth and slides down my throat. This is not something I usually do without my subs wearing a condom. I've never thought semen tasted particularly good. Or at least not until I tasted Damian. He's deliciously bittersweet with a musky tang that resonates through me.

His hands continue running over my hair while I watch the ultimate picture of pleasure transform his face from beautiful to amazing. His cock continues pumping into my mouth. When, at last, he looks down on me, I can't decipher his expression and disappointment swells. He should be shattered like I feel. Instead, he steps back and zips himself carefully inside his pants with little change in his dominant expression. He calmly moves aside and raises the spanking bench until it's higher. With a nod toward the bench, I return to my previous position. I don't think my tender flesh can take more punishment without me safe wording out of this crazy mess. He walks back to the cabinets, removes a dildo and a small black box before situating himself behind me.

"Do I need to restrain your hands?"

Damn, he isn't finished. I will regret this. "No."

His fingers travel to the folds of my pussy—spreading me impossibly wide. I'm so wet the dildo slides in effortlessly. Hell, I think I have enough lubrication to take his entire hand if he forced the issue. He places a Velcro strap around my waist and then between my legs to secure the dildo in place.

"Remember the plug needs to stay in." He walks over to a desk in the corner. The desk was so non-assuming in this den of sin that it went unnoticed until he sat down behind it. He calmly, without seeming to have a care in the world, opens the cover of a laptop and turns it on.

The look on my face must be priceless. He is kidding, right? Keeping my mouth shut at this point is impossible. I open my lips to give him a piece of my mind. He reads me perfectly and presses one long finger on the black box beside the laptop. The vibrator inside my pussy begins humming.

I arch my neck as the pleasure swells deep inside my pussy where the mind-shattering bliss vibrates. My lower belly tightens again. I gasp for air and stop fighting my body. The bastard shuts off the vibrator. Frustration makes me sag back down against the bench.

A few minutes later, I'm back in control and glance across the room. My eyes must be shooting flames.

"How does it feel?" he asks and leans farther back in his chair. "My cock has been hard since the day I met you. You remain unruffled and that tight little ass of yours keeps walking away. You do not have permission to come. I want you suffering."

"You basta…aweg." He turns the switch higher this time. My hips pump against the side of the bench. I can't think past the vibration. Another orgasm is within my grasp. This will make three. Fuck everything. I need this.

And it stops.

I'm going to kill him.

"What, nothing to say?" he taunts.

My body is on fire. No matter that I want to wrap my fingers around his throat and cut off his air supply, I need his cock inside me. Now. I no longer want to play his dominance games but damn I wouldn't mind playing a few of my own. I will handle this myself. I close my eyes and picture him naked, tied to a bed, his long thick cock at attention waiting for my mouth. Slowly, my tongue runs along the length—circling, nibbling, sucking. He's unable to touch me or control my movements and I sit up, raise my body above him, and impale myself on each sweet inch.

The vibrations start again and I plummet over the edge, screaming into the room. The heat in my veins rushes to my pussy and doesn't stop until a hard slap to my already sore derriere brings me back into the now.

"Shame on you. Bad little sub. What were you thinking?"

I open my eyes and turn my head so I'm looking directly into his dark eyes. "You," I say in a breathy post-orgasmic whisper. "I was thinking of your neck between my fingers and pressure. Your face turning blue and your eyes rolling back inside your head. Seconds before you pass out I release my hold and bury my knee deep in your groin." I allow a tight smile. "That, Master Damian, gets me the fuck off."

His laughter is deep and full and does strange things to my wrung out body. He caresses my cheek. "You know you're mine, don't you?"

His words—hot, sexy, and commanding—quiver through me. I'm not his. No. It can't happen. And sadly, a big part of me wants exactly that. While my thoughts swirl, Damian's fingers rub my clit. I'm so fucking sensitive and desire doesn't immediately flare. I've worked so damn hard to establish myself as a Domme. I've dreamed of having my own club for years. Me and Raul. I wasn't taken seriously in the beginning. I don't think Damian's ever taken me seriously. I must fight what he's doing to me.

Whether I want it to or not, my body begins responding—the wet noises from the slide of his fingers doesn't help. My orgasms have a scent that I never noticed and I like it. The taste of Damian is still on my tongue and makes a powerful combination.

He pulls the plug partially out and then moves it back in. I continue fighting and I think I'm winning until Damian's lips press against my back. The warmth of his mouth travels higher and gentle nips follow the wet kisses. He suddenly pulls my braid, lifting my head. His lips take mine and I fall over the edge. Can an orgasm start at your lips? I think it can and the delicious things he's doing to my pussy carry me along. I groan into his mouth while he plays my body like a musical instrument. My world is Damian, his lips and his fingers. I never want this to end.

I fade back into Damian's realm and discover he's removed the toys from my ass and pussy along with the wrist and ankle cuffs. Damn, the nipple clamps are gone too. He lifts me within his strong arms and carries me out of his big glorious dungeon. He gently places me on his large bed. My eyes are barely open, but I watch sleepily as he undresses. He joins me and pulls me into his chest. His fingers unweave my braid and spread the damp strands around us. His touch remains tender while he massages my shoulders and back. Ever so slowly, his hands move down until he's rubbing my red ass and thighs.

His voice is incredibly low when he speaks. "My father started Pleas-Her Toys. He was rarely around when I was a child. He never married my mother but I didn't understand that as a young boy." His hand stops moving and just rests against my fevered flesh. "He had a different woman in almost every state. I still have no idea how many half brothers and sisters I have. He showed up once or twice a year. I would hear my mom's cries of pleasure coming from her bedroom. The few times my dad took me anywhere he would tell me all women were whores. He never used my mom's name but it was implied." Damian's hand squeezes my hip and I don't think he has any idea he's doing it. "I decked him when I was fifteen." His voice changes and I know what he's telling me is an incredibly personal look at what makes him tick. "I pulled his company out from under him five years after I graduated college," he continues. "My father died two years later." Damian hesitates but I don't think he's finished. "My mother still loves him."

The room is quiet except for our combined breathing. I lay quietly thinking about how far out of my element I am. Damian is doing exactly what I love right now. This is the soothing time for a sub and even though we're lying side by side, I'm a puddle at his feet. "Why are you doing this, Damian?" I ask softly and continue before he answers. "You and I won't work and I'm leaving at the end of the month."

"You're so stubborn." I can hear the hurt in his voice but I can't give in. He speaks again before I can stop him and his voice takes on a lighter note. "Now it's your turn," he says and shifts slightly. "Tell me something I don't know about you."

He's killing me. I can't do this. Not the personal stuff. I need to take his mind away from this questioning. I smile wickedly and flick my tongue against his upper arm. His grin answers mine and his beautiful dimples appear as if he understands what I'm thinking. He rolls us until I'm lying on top of him, our legs intertwined. His arms rise and his hands grasp the brass rails of the headboard. "This is for you. Do your worst."

He knows my craving is a ruse, but he lets it go. "Can I tie you?" I ask.

There are tiny gold flakes in his eyes and I swear they're sparkling right now. "No, baby, but I won't let go."

I sit up and rest on his lower thighs. After scooting back a little, I rearrange us so his legs are on either side of me. His body is exceptional—the contours rippled. His hard abs beg for my tongue. His erection stands tall and proud. I need him inside me, but I have a fantasy to play out first.

He's actually enjoying this, which surprises me. "If you need a condom, they're in the nightstand drawer." He nods to my right with a quirk to his lips.

"Oh, I'll eventually need one or two," I tell him with a wink. His cock jumps at the words and my grin widens. Looking up, his dark wicked eyes meet mine. I lean over him and lick his nipple. When it's hard beneath my tongue, I give the other the same attention. It's been a long time since I've wanted to worship a man's body like this. I live in a world where fantasies come true, but I rarely live mine. Right now

I'm taking what I want. I lick and nibble as I move down his chest to the valleyed plains of his abs. His skin is a combination of salt and musk that ramps my own desire up ten notches.

He plays nice and keeps his hands on the rails. His muscled arms tighten when he particularly likes a place I'm touching him. As a Domme, it's up to me to learn about his wants and needs.

I'm not his Domme, I remind myself silently. I lick a wet circle around his belly button and it's easy to allow negative thoughts to drift away. This is about mutual enjoyment, and having Damian beneath me takes joy to an entirely new level. My tongue glides upward, and I don't take my mouth from him until I'm at his collarbone. I rise up a bit and reach into the drawer to remove a condom.

I re-adjust positions so Damian's cock is standing at attention between my thighs. I slide the condom over him, watching his face while I do it. His eyes are barely open and the firmness of his jaw shows how much control he's exerting to keep his hands in place. I lift up on my knees and position his cock at my entrance. Staring into his eyes, I slowly sink down until my pussy surrounds his thick heat.

His hips rock upward, sending an undeniable thrill directly to my pussy. I rest my hands on his chest and his muscles bunch beneath me. I throw my head back as I find my rhythm. It doesn't take long before my lower belly tightens. Damian strains and his breathing grows ragged. His heavy groan fills the room and his cock spasms inside me when he comes. Hot seed fills the condom and even through the latex I feel it. My orgasm rockets over me, traveling along my nerve endings and sending electrical pulses clear to my toes. My ears fill with screams of fulfillment.

It's seconds, minutes, I'm not sure before Damian pulls me down so I'm lying fully on top of him. Our bodies stay joined. I'm not sure I've ever been this sexually satisfied in my life. Damian rolls and disengages his body from mine. I'm too tired to open my eyes when he leaves the bed. A minute later he's back. He pulls me into the comfort of his chest and that's the last thing I remember before sleep takes me away.

    ***

Early morning sunlight slips through the sheer window coverings and wakes me. I'm alone. I inhale the combined scent of Damian and sex. The two go deliciously hand in hand. There's a bathrobe at the foot of the bed. It's not the one from the night before. This is soft, plush terry cloth, and when I put it on, it ends at my ankles. I detour to the bathroom before I go in search of my Dom.

Sitting at the table drinking a cup of coffee and reading the paper, is the last person I expect to see. Carl looks up when I approach.

"Good morning. I've brought some clothes for you and then I'm to escort you back to your rooms. Samson has been walked and fed this morning, and I was told to let you sleep and that you will not be working tonight." His voice carries little inflection.

"Where is he?" I ask while trying to keep the hurt of a missing Damian from my tone.

Carl places the newspaper on the table and rises. "He left on a business trip and should be back in a few days."

My world collapses. Carl avoids my eyes and carries his coffee cup into the kitchen. I glance around and spot the bag he brought. Picking it up, I head in search of another bathroom. I refuse to enter Damian's bedroom again.

The bathroom mirror shows my sleep tousled hair swirling around haunted eyes. Why didn't Damian mention he was leaving today? He could have left a note, anything. The longer I think about it the angrier I become. I jerk on my clothes and leave the bathroom. Carl takes me through the front door to a bank of elevators. These are different from the private one inside his apartment. Carl points out the correct elevator and enters a code when we're inside. The doors open. Carl reaches in front of me and opens another door. We enter a familiar bedroom and Sam's whine on the other side of the bedroom door confirms that we're in my suite.

I look at Carl. "Will my code work on this elevator and take me to Damian's suite?"

Carl glances away. "I don't know. Damian would need to set the access code with your room code."

"I see. Thanks for the escort. I'll see you tonight."

Carl's expression shows he's nonplussed at my announcement. "Damian gave you the night off," he says in a slightly exasperated tone.

My hand swoops out and I motion at the elevator. "When the rat's away the mice will play. I'll see you tonight."

Carl leaves and when I'm sure the elevator has taken him to his destination, I punch my room code into the keypad beside the door. Nothing. I'm locked out of Damian's private world and I'm determined to lock him out of my heart. Mr. Quick Dick will not play me again.

Chapter Twenty-Two

Damian

My cell wakes me. It's Monroe and it's very strange to hear from him so soon. I leave Lydia sleeping and head to my penthouse office so I won't wake her.

"Yeah," I answer with a little more heat than I probably should. Leaving Lydia alone in my bed was not how I planned this morning.

"I have an emergency."

My irritation disappears. "What's wrong?"

"I have two women who need transport. The circumstances are delicate or I wouldn't ask. I need you to handle this personally." I can hear in his tone that this is serious.

Three minutes later, I have details and it's not good. I'm out the door five minutes later. I call my emergency pilot so the plane is ready by the time I hit the airport. I also call Carl to handle Lydia for me. I didn't wake her because my explanation required time, which I didn't have. After learning the two women were in imminent danger, I made the decision to leave Lydia in my bed and explain later.

I would love to see her fiery eyes when she wakes up and I'm not there. That's where my enjoyment ends, though. I would much rather fuck her brains out until neither of us is capable of leaving the bed.

I arrive in Arizona two hours after takeoff. A driver picks me up and takes me to Monroe's location. It's a warehouse in downtown

Phoenix. At least the inside is slightly cooler than the outside. Monroe is waiting with two other men.

"Damian, this is Moon. He will fill you in."

We shake hands and Moon provides further information. "They've been cleared to travel by my personal physician but they're in bad shape. They speak English and won't cause trouble. If the man who had them discovers their location, he'll kill them." His gaze intensifies. "Tell no one but Monroe their location. We should have the situation straightened out in the next forty-eight hours."

While Moon is speaking, I notice the other man's gaze on me. His hands are at his sides at the ready and his legs slightly parted in a stance that allows him to balance perfectly. He screams bodyguard and definitely not someone you mess with.

"I'll stay with them until the *problem* is eliminated," I say. There's no way I'll leave my mom and the other women she's caring for unprotected.

"Thank you," Moon says. I follow him to the back of the warehouse into another room. There's a sink and cabinet to the left. The cement floor dips slightly with a floor drain in the middle of the room. It's not difficult to figure out that I don't want to know what happens in here. A slight noise makes me turn to the right. There are two cots in the corner. Both women sit on the same cot with a single blanket around their shoulders. One has bandages covering her face with only her eyes and mouth showing. The other woman's face is a mass of scrapes and bruises with swollen features that make my hands tighten into fists at my sides. Someone beat the shit out of them. They're also drastically underweight.

Moon approaches the women and speaks to them in Spanish before making introductions. "You'll be safe with Mr. Collins," he assures them. The women rise with the help of Moon's man. They aren't afraid of him, which relieves me somewhat. Both women are wearing long gauzy skirts and loose tops. The skin at their throats and their arms is translucent. They're both shaking as they slowly make their way through the warehouse to the waiting car.

I shake hands with Moon while the other man loads them into the back of the car. I called my mother on my way here, so she's aware she's gaining two extra guests along with her son until the women leave. Moon has no idea where I'm taking them and he's okay with that. Again, I don't want to know the whys. These men navigate a different world than the one I live in.

The trip to the airport and then the flight back to Houston are relatively quiet. I can't help but let my mind wander to the previous evening after we're belted in and taking off.

Lydia.

There's so much I need to explain. She needs to know about this part of my life and why I would leave her after the night we shared. Seeing women in the condition of these two makes me realize how short life actually is. I need and want Lydia in my world and I'm tired of waiting. Going to my mom's will solve one of the problems I have because I'm bringing her on board with my plans. If I can't convince Lydia, my mom will. Never underestimate a mother's need for grandbabies. I smile at the thought of a precious little girl with Lydia's smile and stubborn streak.

"Señor?"

The heavily accented voice makes me open my eyes. The two women are seated across the aisle. "Please call me Damian. May I get you something?"

"We are thankful for your help." The words are slow and meticulous. Her face is so swollen, it's hard to decipher the slight smile she gives me. There are tears in her eyes. I look back and forth between them and I'm angry again.

I control the rising fury and answer gently. "I'm taking you to my mother. She has other women there who come from similar circumstances as you. She'll take care of you and I'll be there to keep you safe until Monroe collects you."

"Gracias, Señor."

"You're welcome." What will Lydia think when I tell her about this part of my life? She has an amazing heart and I expect she'll take the next trip with me. I welcome her help and having a woman along with me will make the transition for these women easier.

After Lydia forgives me for leaving her this morning, we'll have a long talk. She will be mine and I'll be hers. The truth is I'm bored with my life. Not this part where I feel I'm actually helping those in need but the business part. For years, I was driven to best my father. Now I have more money than any person has a right to. I have good managers to keep the business end of my empire turning and I find myself spending more time in the club and handling those business matters myself. The truth is, I enjoy the day-to-day workings of Club El Diablo. It's the only place that I can be myself.

Lydia is the perfect fit. She has so much to offer. I know she wants her own club, and hell, I'll sign Club El Diablo over to her if that's what it takes. I see the way she looks at me. The yearning in her eyes matches my own. Convincing her that she needs me as much as I need her is the problem. If I fail, she'll walk away. Now I know what it means to love a woman. The possibility of losing her is impossible to comprehend. I have my work cut out for me and Mom is my ace in the hole.

A car waits at the airport and I hustle the women inside when we arrive. My mom is waiting with her customary smile when we reach her home. It's an hour before the women are settled and I have a chance to talk to her in private. I make my pitch and end with, "I want you to go back to the club with me and speak to Lydia if I can't get through to her."

For the first time, my mom's gentle smile disappears. "If you can't convince her, you need to let her go, son."

We're in the sitting room, which in my opinion is the most uncomfortable room in her home. I stand and begin pacing. "I can't lose her," I finally say.

Mom pulls a small pillow into her lap and squeezes it into her chest. She hates when I'm unhappy and I have a feeling I won't like what she's about to say. "I know what it's like to be in love without the love reciprocated. Don't make the mistakes I made. Your Lydia sounds incredible, but she's a woman who knows her mind. You need to let her decide." Her smile returns. "I can't imagine that she doesn't love you and you need her stubbornness to counter yours. I'll help you, but if she truly wants to go back to California and her old life, I'll help her do that too. Love takes at least two people to make it work."

I run my hand across my head, stop pacing, and turn. The thought of losing Lydia is not one I want to think about even though I know my mother is right. "I'll let her go if needed, but it won't be easy."

Mom rises and crosses the room until her arms are tightly around me. Her head doesn't even come to my chin. I pull her tightly into my chest and take the comfort she provides. I've never questioned that a woman smaller than me can be dominant and that's due to the small woman I now hold in my arms. My biggest wish is for Lydia to find a place in my world by being exactly who she is. Our time alone and the games we'll play are more than enough for me. I need this to be everything for Lydia.

Holly S. Roberts

Chapter Twenty-Three

Lydia

I open the bedroom door to Sam's exuberant dog kisses. At least he missed me. I lie down on the lush carpet and let him cuddle while I run my fingers through his short black fur.

Then I cry.

I'm not sure how much time passes, when a quiet knock sounds at the front door. I lift myself from the floor and open the door to Raul. He hesitates for only a moment before his arms slip around me. The tears start again.

"Oh, baby," he whispers while rubbing my back with slow circles.

Sobs bubble up from my throat and spill over. Raul lifts me, and my strong submissive friend carries me to the couch where he sits with me on his lap. He places gentle kisses on my head. The truth spills out and I tell him everything about my night with Damian. With a last sniff, I admit I've fallen in love with the damn hell's spawn.

Raul squeezes me tighter. "He loves you too, Lydia. I don't know why he left without a word, but he'll be back. The man has eyes for no one but you. Even when you don't know he's there, he's watching. I'm also smack in the middle of the submissive grapevine and there's a gaggle of angry subs because he's off the market. The man is crazy about you."

Sadly, I'm too mentally fucked up to believe him. I've had so many issues in my life and body image is at the top of the list. I fought anorexia just as Damian accused me of. I still fear my body returning to what it was. I'm weak and a complete sham when it comes to being a Domme. I want a man to love me. Not my body, because I know how weak I am. Damian makes me feel beautiful now. The little fat girl inside wants to always be beautiful in his eyes.

Raul holds me while I cry through the painful what-ifs. When my tears dry, he feeds me and puts me in bed, where I sleep for the better part of the day. When the sun is going down, I shower and dress for work.

The club is the same, but I'm not. I need to finish this contract and get back home to my small apartment and the rest of my life. Our life—mine and Raul's. My eyes sweep the carousel looking for someone to take my mind off my current misery. I'm wearing a black leather corset and skirt, knee-high black boots, and I've left my hair wild and free. I also have on more makeup than usual because my eyes stayed red and puffy no matter how much I worked at being presentable.

After watching the carousel for ten minutes, I ask a shy guy named Tony to sub for me. I review his paperwork and we talk about what he's looking for. He likes extreme pain. His need isn't usually for me, but tonight I try. Halfway through the scene, tears build and finally my arm drops. I look around and see Kyle standing to the side as he had when he joined me for the other scene. I whisper to Tony and ask his permission to hand him off to Kyle, and he thankfully looks relieved. What we had going was not working for either of us. I toss the whip to Kyle and walk away.

Raul approaches before I reach the elevator, but I shake my head in a short, resounding "No." I go back to my room and change so Sam and I can run. We head out of the elaborate front doors of the hotel and take off. Within half a mile, I find my pace and lose myself in the world of breathing, straining leg muscles, and feet pounding the pavement.

When I finally look around, Sam and I are lost. The tall buildings don't look familiar and neither does the street sign I pass. Headlights a short distance away creep slowly toward us and my breath catches at the dangerous situation we're in. Not that Sam can't handle most situations, but I'm mentally kicking myself for this stupidity. By the time the long black limo rolls to a stop, I realize it's Carl and I'm able to breathe again.

The window slides down. "Get in," he says gruffly in a no-nonsense voice that pisses me off.

"I'll walk thank you very much." It would be really stupid to let him pull away without getting directions, but I almost do it. "Could you point me in the right direction before you roll along?"

His jaw sets and it's obvious he isn't happy. "You're not in the best area of town," he grinds out. "Damian will kill me if something happens to you. Get. In."

Oh my. Damian will be unhappy. Too fucking bad. "I think you have me confused with a sub. For your information, I'm not. I'll take care of myself and I have Sam here to protect me."

Carl makes a strangled noise in his throat and I almost think he'll get out of the car and pull a Damian on me. Sam might like him, but if he lays hands on me, it will be a different story. I would hate it if Carl lost an arm, but I'm standing my ground. He stares at me for several long minutes before he sighs. "I'll keep following. I'm armed and won't hesitate to use my weapon if you get yourself into trouble. Their death will be on you."

He's not joking, but fortunately I'm willing to accept the consequences of my actions. I still need time to process what's going on in my head. Carl points his hand to the right and I start walking in the direction he recommends. It's really not his fault that his boss is an asshole. Thankfully, no one stops us. From the strange looks we receive from the few people around at this time, a woman running with a Rottweiler, followed by a limo, is not normal for this area. Once we reach the hotel, I head straight to my room and fall into a deep sleep. I wake up in the afternoon and eat a light meal. My cell has multiple messages from Raul. I send him a text telling him I'll be back at the club for my shift.

I feel bad about the poor sub I turned over to Kyle last night and search for him so I can apologize. Once that's settled, I spend the night working scenes and talking to other dominants. When my shift ends, I go to my room and attempt sleep.

Rinse and repeat, I tell myself the next evening when it's time to work. I'm another day closer to returning home and I use that as my mantra to keep going. I find a submissive who's relatively new to the club. We work out the parameters of the scene and I actually feel a touch of excitement at helping her explore her limits. I start with a deerskin flogger on her thighs and ass. It's soft and has a good pop. The sound is half the fun and her startled scream at the first strike makes me smile. After I have her warmed up, I turn her on the cross and focus on her pussy and breasts. She's responsive. I check on her when tears fall down her cheeks.

"No, please keep going," she hiccups. Like me, she's using this lifestyle to work through her issues and I respect her tears.

The scene continues. I'm fully back in control with my feelings buried deep inside me where they need to stay. I'm not watching the crowd. My focus is all about my sweet new sub. I actually jump when warm hands come around me and pull me back against a hard chest. I don't turn and look because I know who has me. I want nothing more than to sink into his warmth and give in to everything my body needs. I can't, though. I need to guard my heart and put a stop to a certain Dom who's taken the joy from my world.

"Mistress Anna is taking over for you. You need to come with me and not cause a scene," he whispers.

His arms loosen so I can turn but he's still holding me. God, he looks good enough to fucking eat. The cuffs of his white dress shirt are rolled up. He's in dress slacks and not his usual club attire. It takes everything I have not to drop at his feet and rest my head again him. I can't, though. That's not who I am. Or maybe it is who I am with him but he can never know it. "I don't want this. Please let me continue working."

He shakes his head slightly. "No. We can do this the easy or hard way. Your call."

Anna takes the flogger from my hand. She grins slightly without saying anything and I know I won't get any help from her.

"Lydia," Damian says and I turn back to him. "Place your arms around my neck and wrap your legs around my waist." He doesn't give me time to reply before lifting me.

I have no idea what shit he's pulling now. I also have no idea why I comply. I expect him to take me to his office. Instead, he walks past the carousel and stops at the bar. My rear end hits the cold black marbled surface and Damian stands between my fishnet-covered thighs. I'm in another short skirt tonight paired with red stiletto heels and a red corset. I remove my hands from around Damian's neck and wait impatiently for whatever he has planned next.

"Stand up," he says in his Dom voice.

I'm not sure what he means. "What?"

He steps back and bends slightly. He lifts my feet and turns me so my heels land on the top of the bar. "Stand up," he repeats.

He's crazy. I guess I'm crazy too. I stand. Using his arms, Damian lifts himself on top of the bar. Instead of standing, he goes to his knees. His antics are drawing a crowd. He circles my waist and startles me when he pulls me in close until his forehead rests against my belly. I inhale slowly. Even the carousel has stopped spinning and everyone is curiously watching us. Why am I falling under Damian's spell again? It's just not fair.

"What are you doing?" I hiss. God, I think to myself. Please give me a backbone.

Damian leans away and tilts his head so we're looking into each other's eyes. "I want you," he says simply. His voice carries and I'm well aware everyone around us can hear him. "I want you in my bed and in my life, permanently. Tie me up... use me... whatever it takes. I'll lift you up when you need my help. I'll keep you safe and give you everything I have. If that's not enough, I'll sub for you. Don't leave me, Lydia, I love you." Slowly, he pulls a gold club necklace from his pocket. He slips the chain over his head and the heart rests against his heart.

The world stops. The arrogant Dom I met a few weeks ago is on his knees telling me he loves me and proving it. My heart melts and all the threads of my life connect. I have two choices—walk away or go all in. My plan for my own club fades instantly. The simple truth is I can't hold onto my anger or my dreams because those dreams have changed at Damian's words. I step back and sink to my knees. I reach out and finger the heart on his chest. Our eyes remain locked until I lean in and kiss him. I control this kiss because he understands exactly what I need.

"Is that a yes?" he asks when I pull away.

He's a good man—stubborn, aggravating, and dominating. I love him even when I want to punch him for leaving me to wake up alone. I'm not sure when desire for his amazing body and dominant skills turned to this. I'm unaware of my tears until Damian slides his finger across my cheek and wipes them away. "Yes," I whisper in a choked voice.

The dimples I love so much light up his face. "Yes?" he asks with surprise.

"Are you taking it back?" I whisper through my tears.

"Never," he breathes before pulling me in for another kiss. My big bad Dom lets me know who's in charge this time. Our relationship is a two-way street. Both of us can give and take. When he needs it, I'll happily flip him over my shoulder and put him in his place. As the kiss continues, our audience breaks into applause with a few cheers thrown in.

"Can we go somewhere private?" I ask breathlessly when the kiss ends. The fact that Damian shared this moment with these people is amazing. They're part of his world and as I look into their smiling faces, I realize they're part of mine too.

Damian's expression changes to a guilty smile. "My mother is upstairs and she wants to meet you."

"What?" I must not have heard him correctly.

His grin changes and merriment fills his eyes. "I brought her with me so she could talk sense into you if you turned me down."

He can't be serious. "You brought your mother here?"

"If waiting in my apartment is here, then yes, I did."

I'm no longer smiling. "You're insane," I say while trying to control my temper. I can't meet his mother right now. I might be wearing proper club attire but on the street, I'd look like a prostitute.

He ignores my horror at the thought of meeting his mother right now. "Come on." He jumps down and places his arms up. I grasp his shoulder when he lifts me off the bar. Once my feet are on solid ground, I release him and put my hands on my hips. "I'm not meeting your mother dressed like this."

He only laughs. "I told her I might be bringing you bound, gagged, and over my shoulder. She was in the lifestyle and probably still is, but I don't want to picture it please. You'll love her and she'll love you. She always wanted a daughter."

I can't believe what I'm hearing. And it doesn't change that I'm not meeting his mother until I'm dressed appropriately. My anger is building because like he's done repeatedly, he isn't listening to me. "Look, Mr. Manipulative, I—" Damian cuts me off by swinging me over his shoulder in a move too quick and unexpected for me to stop him. Clapping breaks out again and my upper body dangles. "I'm going to kill you," I yell so everyone can hear. His deep laughter is what I get for my effort.

He sets me down in front of the personal elevator in his office. Without entering the code, he steps into me and my back hits the elevator door. His arms come up and rest on either side of my head. "You're beautiful, though my mom won't care if you had two heads and crossed eyes on both of them. I told her I would bring you back within thirty minutes. I don't lie to my mother. She wants to share what an incredible little boy I was and what a great husband and father

I'll make. If you absolutely can't meet my mother dressed as the person you truly are, say so now and I'll wait for you to change clothes." He ends this statement with a soft kiss.

Hell, what do I have to lose? This *is* who I am.

Holly S. Roberts

Chapter Twenty-Four

Lydia

Damian's mother is everything he promised and more. She's asked me to call her Mom or Dixy. The only similarities in the two are their matching dimples. She's wearing a loose flowing gauzy dress similar to the ones I prefer when I'm not in the club. She's plump in a soft hugs kind of way and she immediately puts me at ease.

She reaches up and pinches Damian's cheek after the introductions. "My boy here is smitten with you and thought he would need my help convincing you that he's a good catch." Damian groans and rolls his eyes. "None of that, young man. I'm about to point out that you have your faults but any woman would be crazy to turn down the opportunity to train you," she says with a little added steel in her voice that makes me smile.

I give a nervous laugh because she clearly has Damian's stubbornness. "I'm sorry for not changing before meeting you. Your son seemed to think he was on a schedule."

She takes my hands in hers and looks me up and down before commenting. "You're lovely, dear. I care more about the woman on the inside, though. Once we're acquainted, you'll be even more beautiful to me." Her grin widens and she gives Damian another pointed look before leaning in and kissing my cheek. She may be bossy with Damian but there's no doubt she loves him. She's the perfect mother of the devil because she doesn't take his crap.

"Sit down with me. You and I have much to discuss." We sit in the living room and she immediately continues. "I fear I'm getting frail with age and the only answer is grandchildren. They say babies increase life expectancy in the elderly and I could really use some help."

"Mother," Damian drags out the word.

"Hush. Lydia has a right to know that I want grandchildren and I won't be quiet about it."

Damian shakes his head and gives me a wink. "Don't listen to her, she can outwalk a migrating buffalo."

"See what I put up with?" Dixy adds with her own eye roll. Damian doesn't stop her from her mission, though. "How many children do you want and how soon do you plan on working on the first one?"

I snap my jaw closed when I realize it's hanging open. "Damian and I haven't discussed children." Or for that matter marriage, but I don't say that out loud. "Not that I mind them," I tell her quickly.

"Good, good. I expect the two of you to discuss this shortly so I have some answers. I can be patient to a point. I also expect you to show me around Damian's club. He's been averse to giving me a tour and I've asked for years. If I knew the damn private code, I would go myself." She doesn't give me a chance to answer. "Tell me something about yourself, Lydia. My son was stingy on details."

I stumble a bit with a short biography. Her questions dig out more information. I like her directness, and the fact that she puts Damian in his place is a bonus.

An hour later she abruptly turns to her son. "Take her to bed and celebrate life. I'm tired and need my beauty sleep." She turns back to me and there's no way I can hide my pink cheeks. "We'll go shopping tomorrow and enjoy private girl time. I have so many stories to tell you about this rascal." She smiles at Damian, stands, and literally shoos us from the room to go have sex. I might sink to the floor directly below Damian's penthouse.

Did I mention how perfect she is?

I'm sure it's for his mother's benefit when Damian scoops me up and carries me off. I wave goodbye to Dixy over his shoulder and receive her biggest grin yet. I'm relieved when we bypass the dungeon and he takes me to his bedroom. The dungeon would be more than I can handle after my first meeting with Dixy. I have no doubt she would be delighted to see us enter the dark delights of Damian's private dungeon, though. I doubt much shocks her.

Damian places me on my feet at the foot of his bed. "What would you like, sweet Lydia?"

I circle my hands around his neck. "I want you."

"Good answer," he replies huskily. "Your call. Are you up for a little vanilla or do you want me tied to the bed? I'm all yours."

A thrill shoots straight to my pussy at the thought of tying Damian to the bed. I know him, though. "You really don't want me tying you up, do you?"

His eyes stay on mine. "No, but I trust you. If it turns you on, I'm willing to meet you halfway."

It's time to share my biggest secret. I'm nervous but hold his gaze. "I'm a Domme. I'm not a switch or sub to be controlled in or out of your club." The next part is so hard but I go for broke. "What I am is submissive in the bedroom to the right man. I just need to know you'll respect me in my dominant role too." I need him to say it so bad. I must know if he can honor this part of me.

His eyes burn into mine for the longest moment. Suddenly, he reaches up and grabs a fistful of my hair, jerking my head back and taking my lips in one dominant move. His tongue invades and within thirty seconds I'm left gasping for air when the kiss ends. "What turns you on, Lydia? Not the shit in your paperwork or the rules we went over the other night. I want to know everything and I promise to give it to you. What we have in here is private. I will respect you as a Domme and I know I haven't done it as fully as I should have. You turned my world upside down the first night we met. I've been walking on uneven ground since. I might need a reminder every so often, but I know you're capable of giving it to me." His dimples show and my heart flutters.

I won't deny myself any longer. Damian deserves the truth. "I want you as my Dom in the bedroom and everything that goes with it. Master me, drive me crazy, and love me without limits."

He growls deep in his throat and reaches forward to unbuckle my corset. When the last clip snaps open, he tosses the material aside and removes the remainder of my clothes. "Knees," he says in his dominant voice that makes my legs go weak. I drop to my knees and gaze up. My entire body shivers in anticipation of what's to come. He walks to his walk-in closet and disappears. A minute later he comes out with several neckties in his hands. "On the middle of the bed. Ass up."

Damian knows what he's doing and I also trust him to know what I need. Watching him work with subs has opened my eyes to the dominance that leaks from his pores. I've also seen his tender caring side. I have no doubt he cares about the people in his club. I also know he cares about me. I see the question on his face when I don't immediately get on the bed.

"What will you do if I disobey?" I ask coyly.

Fire sizzles in his gaze. "I have a nice large butt plug for naughty subs. We also need to discuss the fact that I won the last bet and you owe me."

"You didn't win that bet, I had…" I count in my head quickly and it dawns on me that he's right. I completely forgot that stupid wager and I somehow miscalculated my orgasms. His finger on my lips stops me from speaking. "You have two seconds to get on that bed."

My scramble off the floor to the bed is in no way elegant and I don't even care. The thrill running through me makes my body heat up for what's to come. I don't stop until I'm on my hands and knees in the middle of the bed like ordered.

"Chest down, arms spread."

Once I'm in his desired position, he loops the neckties around my wrists and attaches them to the edges of the headboard. Now my ass is really in the air. I've never allowed a man to do this to me and I'm so damn ready.

"Spread your legs wider," he commands.

The bottom of the bed dips when I comply. I'm not expecting his tongue on my pussy, and it startles me. Damian pinches my ass. "Your job is to remain still while I enjoy this amazing pussy. If you come, I'll add to the punishment you have coming."

"Wha—" I try to ask but he stops with a stinging slap on my ass. His tongue and mouth go back to work driving me crazy. A few minutes later he adds his fingers and I almost go off. He reads me too well and backs away. The bed bounces slightly when he stands. I'm a quivering mess and not happy he's left me in this condition. I'm startled again when a bottle of lube lands in front of my face.

Damian's hand smooths down my back. "Your call, Lydia, but this is what I want. It's one of your hard limits and not one I'm happy about. I'll abide by your limits, but I need to know you want this entirely off the table."

I stare at the lube. "No, no limits," I groan.

He slides on a condom before picking up the lube to liberally squirt it on his cock. My nerves are keeping me from enjoying the sight of him rubbing his erection with the silky lube. He moves behind me and comes up over my back. He adds lube to his hand and slides a finger into my ass. It doesn't hurt and I know from working with my subs that I need to relax. I inhale and exhale deeply while Damian readies me. Two fingers are slightly uncomfortable. Damian uses his other hand to play with my clit. "You've got this, baby. Don't fight it."

He pulls his fingers out and the head of his cock pushes against me. The ache is almost unbearable and I come close to using my safe word. He pushes slowly past the nerves at my entrance and stops long enough for me to inhale deeply. With another push, Damian slides fully inside me, and I yell into the room. Damian's hand pushes against the center of my back so he has leverage to fuck my ass. He pushes in slow and pulls out just as slowly. The ache goes to a burn because I don't think I can hold back my pending orgasm.

"I'm going to come," I gasp.

"No, you'll wait for me." He increases his tempo and I can do nothing but absorb his domination as he takes his pleasure. I'm at the end of my endurance when he goes off. My cry joins his and I come undone.

Damian collapses on my back and removes the looped ties from my hands. We're still breathing hard when he leaves the bed and disposes of the condom. He's back immediately and wraps me in his arms facing him.

"You're my everything, baby," he whispers. I'm safe and no longer at a crossroads. I open my eyes and Damian is studying me. "You owe me a secret. That's what I want for the bet you lost."

He deserves my secrets. I want all of his. It takes a moment to gather my thoughts and I appreciate that he doesn't rush me. "I'm sure you know my father was a jockey." Damian nods. "He was short and thin. His size never took away from how tough he was when riding. I was so proud to be his daughter." I hesitate knowing this next part will be hard. "It would have been easier if my mom was alive while I was growing up. My dad hung out with other jockeys. Our world consisted of little people like my father. Next to them, I was a giant. My father told me he was attracted to my mother because of her lush curves, but I didn't really believe him. Sure, I had pictures of him and my mom but for some reason I only saw her beauty and never compared my body to hers. When I looked in the mirror, I saw a fat blob. Even the daughters of the rich horse owners were thin and gorgeous. My father died and my world turned upside down. I was seventeen and only because I had a decent job at the local horse track did child services stay off my back. I had no one to live for and I was so damn young."

Fuck. I've talked to multiple therapists about what I went through and this should be easier than it is. "I tried to starve myself to death and almost managed it. I finally collapsed and was hospitalized. I was diagnosed with anorexia and bulimia." I breathe slow and deep. Damian runs his hand over my thigh and I appreciate his compassion. "With the help of therapy, I found a balance and used exercise to keep my demons at bay." I need him to understand that I will always fight these demons much like an alcoholic fights theirs. "I'm borderline now. The kink world helps me with body image, but when I look in the mirror," I close my eyes and finish the sentence, "I still see the fat girl." I still can't look at Damian while saying the rest. "I use control as a Domme to control myself, not others. As long as I'm in charge, I can fight the need to eat and throw up or the need to stop eating." There, it's out. He knows I'm a fake and that the possibility is there for me to falter.

"Look at me, baby."

I open my eyes and Damian wipes the tears from my cheek. "You're a Domme because it's what's inside you. I've watched you. I watch the people who respond to you. That can't be faked and neither can your dominance." He smiles gently. "Not many people can stand up to me when I use the tools in my arsenal. You did. What we do here in the bedroom is between us and no one else. You can get your Domme on any time you choose. If you choose submission in here, I'll cherish every minute." He lifts my hand and kisses the backs of my fingers. "Love comes in all shapes, sizes, and kinks. My love is about what's inside here." He releases my hand and places his between my breasts. My heart beats against his palm and I exhale the breath I've been holding.

"I love you," I tell him.

"You kept me waiting," he teases.

"I didn't want to say it until you knew everything and decided to keep me."

His deep laugh fills the room. "You should know by now that I go after what I want. After the crazy chase you took me on I'm not letting you go."

"Do you want children?" I ask because his mother was so persistent.

He slides his hand down to my stomach. "I want a child here. I want to see you round with my baby and tease you when you think you're too fat. You never will be even if you're five times the size you are now. I love what's in here." His other hand goes to my forehead and he gently smooths his thumb across it. "I love what's in here." His other hand travels down until he's cupping my pussy. "My mother can wait. Don't let her pressure you. She'll back off if you're firm about doing this on our timetable. I have no problem waiting until you're ready. We have years to work out all the details for our life."

His kiss is gentle but he's still cupping my pussy. He slides a finger inside. It's me who turns the kiss in another direction. I need this man inside me again and judging by his erection against my hip, he wants the same thing.

There's something to be said about vanilla sex now and then. Damian shows me how much he loves me in a way as old as time. I'm gasping for air when I say, "Ten babies. That's my limit."

He laughs and kisses me again. I swear I would give this man anything he asked for when he's fucking me. "Is that a bet? If so, I want ground rules. I think I can do that in ten years, but if you need them faster, I'll do my best."

"You have your work cut out for you, Mr. Super Semen."

Our combined laughter fills the room. Our life together will never be boring.

Damian and Lydia's story continues with the birth of their first child in the next pages. It's Damian's point of view. Keep reading...

Chapter Twenty-Five

One year later…

Damian

The club is crowded and one problem after another takes me away from my wife. Lydia is expecting our first child and I would rather be doing something kinky, watching television, or even playing a game of chess rather than settling disputes over which sub belongs to whom.

When I'm not around, Lydia has a way of getting into trouble or at least doing things I expressly forbid. I laugh at the thought. "Forbid" is considered the "F" word as far as she's concerned. I learned that the hard way. Now, with her advanced pregnancy, I'm doing my best to use gentle persuasion. The damn woman makes it hard.

Our relationship morphed from two dominants, madly in love, with me controlling our life in the bedroom to a tricky D/s relationship when we aren't in the club. The change has been gradual and somehow we've made it work. Lydia is an incredible Domme and she needs *her* time in order to stay mentally balanced. She also desires domination and we've managed to navigate the sometimes stormy waters and do what works for us. Lydia knows my handprint on her ass works for me and I understand her need to control when we're in the club. She's rocked my world since the moment I saw her picture for the first time and I wouldn't take away one day of our unusual relationship. Can I define it as D/s? For us it is. My dominance has moved out of the bedroom and into our everyday lives. At least when we're outside the club. When we enter the doors of Club El Diablo, Lydia is all Domme and a damned good one.

I glance around the low-light interior of the main room. It's getting late and I need to pick up a few things from my office before returning to my seriously chubby and hotter than hell wife. I open the office door and come to a stop. How she managed to tie herself up stumps me for a moment.

"Mommy's been bad, Sir, and needs a spanking." Her wicked smile tells me just how bad she's been.

"Oh, she has, has she?" I leer in my best Dom voice.

With her largely rounded tummy, there is no way she could lean over the desk for a nice spanking. She's tied to my high-backed office chair with her legs secured wide apart strapped to a spreader bar. Yeah, she had help and I'd bet our kinky scene that it was Raul. Tape binds her hands to the chair arms and a pink ribbon surrounds her stomach with a large pink bow slightly to the side of her outy belly button.

The bulge of her stomach keeps my gaze from her smooth pussy. I may need her to slide forward a bit to see it. I know her pussy is smooth because for the past two months, I've been the one to shave it. My lovely Domme wants a master in bed and that parts easy. It's the in-between times like now that make my dick the hardest. She tries topping me every chance she gets. It's in her blood and God is she sexy when she does it. Like right now, telling me what she needs, and how she needs it. From her chubby cheeks to her swollen hands and ankles she's almost more than I can handle at the moment. I would usually punish her for this behavior, but with her rounded belly she has me twisted around her little finger. The upside is I plan to keep it this way and get her pregnant as many times as she's willing.

A spark flashes in her eyes over my hesitation. "Is Daddy afraid Mommy will make him cry when he comes?" she taunts like the she-devil she is.

I shake my head and cross my arms. She's beyond pushy today and must be suffering. "Make me cry, huh?" I say while trying to keep the smile off my face at her feistiness.

Her voice turns petulant and I continue fighting a grin. "Your mind is a million miles away while your fat wife is displayed in all her glory. I think I'd like to make you cry."

I laugh because I know it pisses her off. I walk closer and lean into the chair putting my lips to her ear. "You know when you use the word 'fat' your Dom only punishes you harder."

"I've been very bad, Sir, and need a heavy hand."

She's laying it on thick. I bite my lip to keep from laughing again. "You promised me you would rest. Having yourself tied up in my office is not resting." I lick the side of her neck and trail my tongue up to her ear. She gives a sexy sigh when I nip her earlobe. I smell her musky arousal and it makes my dick thicken. "You think I'm that easy?" I bite a little harder. "You, my naughty little wife, will not enjoy this." I don't give her a chance to respond. Turning the chair, I wheel her to the wall of my office and push her as far into the corner as she can comfortably fit.

"What are you doing?" she huffs in indignation.

Someone's angry, but this is what she gets for topping from the bottom. It's not my fault she pushes boundaries and has punishment bruises across her ass to prove it. Or at least she did up until about six weeks ago when her belly grew so big. I worry about hurting her, and our sexual antics have been on the tame side recently. Is that what this is about? We'll see. "Well, my disobedient sub, these are my rules: You will not speak unless you want a ball gag in that dirty mouth of yours. You will not have an orgasm until I give you permission. And last, you *will* scream loudly throughout your coming punishment. If—" I let that sink in for a moment. "I decide to grant you the punishment you so rightly deserve."

She strains her neck and looks over her shoulder to glare. "I think Sir has lost his fucking marbles." Yeah, something's obviously got her panties in a twist because she's pushing hard. Her dirty mouth causes her endless trouble and right now is no different. I walk to my desk and take out one of several ball gags I've purchased this past year. This one's new because the others are missing. It took me a while to figure out that she hides them. I'm now playing her game; I hide them until I need one. We've been working on her potty mouth because a child doesn't need to hear the fire she unleashes when she's angry. A ball gag was a last resort, but it's the one that seems to work.

She's watching me and I'm proud of her for not begging. If looks could kill, I'd be lying on the floor in need of resuscitation. I walk closer and run my nose over the skin of her throat. "If you kiss me first, I'll take the gag out sooner," I coax.

Merriment lights her eyes. "You're getting soft," she laughs huskily. "Put those lips to mine so I can fuck your mouth." She dares to use her Dom voice in order to gain back some of her control. Spinning the chair, my lips claim hers. Our tongues tangle as I deepen the kiss. She sucks at my lips and adds more than one gentle nip. There's no one in the world who kisses like she does. I pull away and place my hand on her extended belly. "Is there anything you and

Abigail aren't ready for?" I ask seriously, stopping the scene for a moment because I know we need to be cautious.

"Leave her out of this. Mommy needs to come, and Sir needs to make fucking sure it happens," she snaps.

It's time to take the feisty out of her. If she wants to come and needs me to do it, she will act her part. I lift the small red ball to her mouth and secure the soft leather behind her head. "You look so damn sexy like this. Having you unable to speak or tell me what you want is only icing on the mommy cake. You're perfect." Her eyes go from sensual to snappy just like I knew they would. "You've been resisting my punishments for long enough and building quite the list of transgressions. After Abigail is born, it will be your fault my hand is red and swollen from spanking your ass. Now be a good little sub and work on patience."

I turn the chair so she's facing the corner again. She doesn't start kicking the wall until I've been at my desk looking at paperwork for about three minutes. "Each kick adds five minutes to the time you spend contemplating your lack of subservience."

She screams behind the gag but stops kicking the wall. I go back to my paperwork without really seeing what's in front of me. I'm too conscious of the woman tied up in the corner. She sits without moving for another five minutes and I finally walk over and turn her around. "I have something special planned, so be good." This time I make sure she sees my grin. "Since your mouth is under control, you'll use your fingers if this is too much. One finger means you're close to your limit and two means stop." My hand trails over her delightfully chubby knuckles resting on the arm of the chair. I physically lift one finger from the armrest and then two. "Do you understand?"

I'm unsurprised when her middle finger comes up.

Chapter Twenty-Six

Damian

The items I need are in the cabinet on the far side of the room. I've actually been planning this for some time. I remove three candles, their holders, a lighter, and a medium-sized knife in its sheath. I rest them on the desk. Lydia's eyes have darkened and her breathing is coming in short heavy bursts at the sight of what I have planned.

"Mommy's been bad and Daddy knows the perfect punishment," I tell her. "I've missed clamping these," I gently squeeze one nipple before moving to the other and giving it the same treatment. "I know they're sensitive," I say when her eyes widen. "But I think this will give us what we both want." A small bit of saliva runs down the corner of her mouth and I wipe it with my finger. Licking the wetness away adds a bit of devilment to my plans. "You always taste so good no matter where it comes from."

She closes her eyes for a moment and I know she's fighting to control her dirty needs. During this past year I've learned many of her nuances and plan on sixty more years to learn them all. My sweet wife loves it dirty and though she still fights it in certain ways, she aches for domination.

I light the candles and place them in the holders. "I need you to move your ass a little more forward in the chair to see if our baby is comfortable that way."

She nods.

"Good girl." I kneel between her legs and grasp her hips. "Lift just a bit." I pull her bottom toward me so she's propped slightly back in the chair. I unbutton my black shirt and remove it while she watches. I walk to my desk, remove a hair tie from a drawer in my desk, and then move behind her chair to gather her thick red hair and tie it back. It's hard to believe her hair is actually thicker than before she became pregnant but it is. I place the band around the heavy strands and let it hang down her back in a single ponytail. Moving to the side, I press one of the levers on the chair so it reclines straight back and she's now looking up at me.

"With pain there is always pleasure," I whisper huskily after resting back on my calves and admiring her pussy, which is now visible. I lick one finger and slide it across the folds of her cunt. I tease slowly over her clit and slip my finger inside her tight sheath when she sucks in a breath and doesn't release it. Lifting my finger, I show her the clear silky wetness before licking it off. "You're both sweet and spicy at the same time. There's no taste on earth quite like you. We've only just started, so don't forget to breathe." I smile wickedly and go back to work on her pussy. After a minute of rubbing and teasing, her hips lift off the chair. I bend forward and kiss her stomach and then untie the bow and unwrap my gift. Lifting my hands, I cup the underside of her breasts. I lick one nipple before moving to the other. My thumb circles the moisture I left on her other breast.

"When our baby arrives, she will be sharing her morning feeding with Daddy. I could come right now thinking about how your milk will taste."

Her breathing becomes more erratic and I release her breasts and slide my hands down past her stomach between her thighs again. With one finger, I slowly ease into her pussy while watching the sweet torment on her face until she can't take it any longer and closes her eyes. I know her. I know she's concentrating on touch alone to get herself off quickly. Bad sub. I continue sliding my finger inside her and reach for a candle with my other hand. Leaning forward, I wet the tip of her breast with my mouth again and then spill the first drop of red wax directly on her nipple.

A low moan comes from behind the gag when she feels the heat. I pay attention to her hands as they clench the chair tighter, but she doesn't signal that this is too much. My finger continues assaulting her pussy and I add to it by rubbing my thumb across her clit. I blow gently on the wax and help it cool before repeating the process on her other nipple.

Lydia watches me decorate her breasts with dreamy desire in her eyes. I add blue wax to the mix while keeping the same steady, slow glide of my finger going inside her. Her hips push up insistently. She has trouble remembering who's in charge, and delaying her orgasms is the only way to control her. I continue moving my finger slow and steady. A minute later, she can no longer control herself and grinds into my hand, so I pull my finger away.

"After the baby is born and you're healed, I'll strap your hips down so I can play for a few hours without your interference," I tease. Her eyes open and even without words, I clearly see her need.

The blue wax on her nipple is taking a different path than the red. I use a little more and watch the wax glide down in sensual trails. She's a work of art but then she always has been. Now that her attention is on her breasts, I slide my finger back inside her. Our eyes lock. Her breathing accelerates and a fine sheen of sweat breaks out on her skin.

Her loud groan when I remove my hand from between her legs goes straight to my cock. She bucks her hips in frustration until my hand settles on her shoulder. "Shh, you're doing great. Let me get this off of you." I untie the gag and wipe her mouth with my hand. Her trembling lips beg to be kissed. "Do you have anything to say before we proceed, my dear?"

"I'm dying here," she whines.

"You're so impatient."

Sparks flare in her eyes. "I need to come, dammit. I've needed you all day but you stayed away and left me on my own." Yeah she even pouts in a sexy manner. "I want your cock buried deep in my ass, sliding in and out slowly while your hands squeeze my breasts."

I inhale sharply at the picture she paints. The little minx is teasing me so she gets her way. My damn pants grow uncomfortable as my cock swells. They're suddenly too tight, and the best way to handle this new development is to take them off. Lydia watches with a small smirk. Or at least she does until I take myself in hand and stroke from tip to balls. The smirk disappears and she licks her lips.

"I want to taste, Sir."

Now she's throwing out the big guns because she thinks she's taken back her control. "I haven't properly punished a bad mommy yet." I continue rubbing myself and finally glance up when a bead of cum wells at the head of my cock. I wipe it with my finger before placing it to her lips. "Suck," I whisper.

She sucks my finger until I pull it away. "I hate you."

"No, my love," I tell her gruffly. "You love everything about me." I look down at her breasts and pick up the yellow candle. "I love everything about you too and right now your breasts need more care."

The yellow takes on a life of its own when I drip it over the other wax. It's light enough to pick up the other colors. I step back and admire my handiwork. She's so damn beautiful this way and we'll be repeating this scene when I can use her entire body as a canvas. Wax pooling across her ass is another fantasy I'm determined to fulfill.

Chapter Twenty-Seven

Damian

I stroke her pussy again and build her desire to a boiling point. "Are you close, my dear?"

"God, yes. Please." Pulling my hand away this time is beyond cruel and I fully expect the coming tantrum. "What are you doing?" she screams.

I shake my head to let her know I'm not falling for her antics. "It's time to remove the wax." I lift the sheathed knife off my desk and slide it from the case.

"Oh, hell no! You are not putting that knife near my breasts."

She fights my control so hard, and anytime we try something new she's the bratty sub. "Trust me," I say while holding her gaze. I see the fear and know she gets a thrill out of scenes like this too. She can always use her safe word but I know she won't. Her resistance is part of her sexual make up.

She closes her eyes and I kiss her cheek with a gentle swipe of lips. The knife is dull but half the fun is her not knowing that. I lift her breast in my left hand and pull the skin tight with my thumb before sliding the edge of the knife between the wax and her flesh. She doesn't move, but her eyes open and she stares at the knife as it slides across her skin. Slowly wax curls beneath the blade and falls away.

I finish the first breast and move to the other. With a loud sigh she leans her head back and relaxes while I play. When finished, I remove a bottle of massage oil and a soft cloth from the cabinet across the room. Lydia is calm now, breathing slowly, and in what for her is sub space. I massage the oil into her breasts and allow her the quiet time she needs.

"We're finishing this upstairs," I tell her softly. "I think you need some additional stimulation."

Her eyes peel open. "Hurry," she moans.

I cut the tape on her arms with scissors and remove the spreader bar last. Using a blanket from the kink cabinet, I cover her before lifting her into my arms.

"I keep telling you you're going to break your back."

"Only if you squirm. Now hush and be still."

I walk into the private elevator and press the button for the penthouse. She isn't heavy at all and even pregnant, she fits perfectly in my arms. I increase my stride once we're off the elevator and carry her straight to our bed.

I lay her gently on the comforter. "Remove the hair from the band and then get on your knees with your ass in the air." I turn and head to the dresser without waiting to see if she does as ordered. She won't like the consequences if she disobeys.

When I turn back to the bed, I take a moment to admire well-rounded globes displayed for my pleasure. In three strides I'm close enough to add the key ingredient they're missing. My palm lands with a resounding slap on one cheek.

"What was that for?" she complains.

"For being naughty and because my handprint looks so good on your skin." The next slap lands on her other ass cheek. Her head goes down in submission. I crawl onto the bed behind her and grabbing one of the pillows beside her, situating it under her so she doesn't grow too uncomfortable too quickly. I ignore her grumble and rub my thumbs over the red hand prints I've decorated her ass with. Bending forward, I lick the marks with long sweeps of my tongue. She shivers beneath my touch and hums deep in her throat.

She squirms naughtily as I continue, and I nip her flesh. "Hold still," I order.

"You're killing me. Fuck my ass and get it over with."

"You know that's not happening until after the baby's born, but I have a toy that will help your suffering. I'm deciding if you've earned it and so far you're falling short."

"Please," she groans. We spoke with her obstetrician about our lifestyle. A lot of our play has toned down, but I've found that delaying some of our kinky play gives us so much to look forward to. Her hormones add a wilder streak to her kink and she's been insatiable. For a woman who listed anal sex as a hard limit in the beginning of our relationship, she loves it as much I do now even though we can't do it.

I rest back on my knees and pick up the lube. I liberally poor it on my hand and the plug. Her rounded ass is my favorite place to play. I spread her cheeks and slide my finger along the crevice. With one greased finger, I push past the tight muscle of her asshole and massage in and out. Her muscles grasp my finger and Lydia moans again, her breath growing more erratic. She's doing her best to hold back her little sounds of ecstasy so I won't stop.

"Hold on, baby," I tell her when I remove my finger and slide the small plug into place. My own patience is now at an end and I need to be balls deep inside my wife. Grabbing her hips, I squeeze those extra love handles she hates. They're so fucking sexy and I still don't think she understands what they do to me. I slide my cock home and find the warmth I've been seeking since seeing her tied up in my office. Hell, this is what I've craved since the first time I set eyes on her in that sleazy sex club. She's my mate, my heart, my life.

"Ahhh," she cries as I increase the tempo of my thrusts.

My voice is ragged. "Scream for me, baby. I want to hear you."

"Faster!" she groans.

I pull out and slide my hand against her clit, using the other to move the plug. "Your cunt is so fucking hot around my cock, but you need to give me those sweet sounds I love to hear."

My finger continues circling her clit as I slide back into her warmth. She rests her head on her forearms and finally gives me the submission I've been waiting for. She's a vessel for my pleasure and I need to hear how my dick feels inside her. The sounds she starts making turn me on even more. I increase my thrusts and pinch her clit with each forward push. She sobs with her need to orgasm and the noise sends electrical sparks through my cock and balls.

I can't deny either of us any longer. "Come for me, sweet Lydia."

She buries her mouth in the curve of her arm to stifle her screams. I grab her hair and pull her head back. "I want to hear you. Don't make me stop and punish your naughty ass," I grunt. Stopping now will punish us both. Her screams echo off the walls and take me over the edge.

Her breathing is coming in short gasps when she collapses forward and I roll slightly so I don't squish her stomach into the bed. I remove the plug while she's still overcome by her orgasm and toss it on a towel I left on the nightstand. I shift us slightly and pull her backside into my chest. My fingers trail over her abdomen and I lovingly kiss her shoulder, nuzzling her hair out of the way so my nose rests against her skin. I love the smell and taste of her skin after we make love.

She needs sleep, but I can't stop touching her. Finally, her soft snores rumble from her chest. I've never mentioned her snoring to her, which came with the baby weight. It would bother her and I don't want her worrying or changing anything. I slide my arms from beneath her and roll slightly to get off the bed.

"Don't leave me," she demands sleepily.

Placing a soft kiss on her brow I whisper, "I'm taking a quick shower and then I'll tuck you in with Alexander and join you."

"K, don't forget ATG." She's barely coherent and I place another soft kiss on her shoulder.

Alexander the Great is her five foot feather pillow that offers the most comfortable way for her to sleep. She named the damn pillow for some reason and now shortens the name to ATG. I've put it down to pregnancy peculiarities. I shower and then go to the closet and grab her bright pink ATG. Carrying the monstrosity to the bed, I squish the softness between her thighs and up against her breasts and then join her beneath the covers, pulling her and ATG tightly against my chest. With a last tender smile beneath her shroud of hair, I fall asleep to the sound of her gentle snores.

Chapter Twenty-Eight

Damian

A long hot tongue and dog breath wake me from a sound sleep. Samson must have stayed the night with Raul and now he's back. The damned dog has everyone in his life wrapped around his paws. I push him back so I can untangle myself from the covers and get up. Sam gives a short whine when he looks at his mistress buried beneath the covers; I call him so he doesn't wake her. Raul is sitting at the kitchen table drinking coffee and reading my newspaper when I walk out in a bathrobe.

"Make yourself at home why don't you," I grumble. "Hand over the business section," I add with my hand out. I'm fully aware most people no longer read an actual newspaper but I love it. At least when it's neat and in its proper order.

Raul knows my bark is worse than my bite in the morning. "I haven't been kicked out yet, so the little seduction scene last night must have worked."

I rub my cock and balls to Raul's delight. "The further advanced her pregnancy gets the hornier she becomes. She hasn't done a scene at the club in two weeks. I may be chafed raw in a few more days."

"You could be the only man on earth who complains about a situation like that."

I can't contain my grin. "Believe me that's not a complaint." Raul's laughter joins mine. "Did you by any chance let Sam out to do his business?"

Raul rubs a hand across his jaw. "He's been walked and fed. I lost a bet with your wife and he's mine at night until the baby's born."

My burst of laughter startles Samson, who is lying on the floor a few feet away. He stands up, circles twice, and settles back down. "You haven't learned betting is futile against Lydia?"

"You bet against her all the time."

"Yes, but I cheat." I wink. "All the time."

"She'd kill me if she thought I cheated."

"You're probably right," I answer smugly because I don't lose bets with anyone, including my wife. If I can't win, I don't bother. "Do you think you could handle things at the club for a few weeks after the baby's born?"

Raul appears startled by my question. "Yours could be the only BDSM club in the country run by a sub."

"We're only four floors away and if there's need for me to come down, I'll be sure to pound a few heads."

"Bran will be back from his honeymoon soon. He sent me an email last night. If you don't mind, I'll ask him to give me a hand so we don't need to bother you. It will also save you from head knocking lawsuits."

"Between the two of you, I know you can handle it." Bran married my baby sister, who recently came into our lives. She was one of my father's offspring who I wasn't aware of until she showed up.

"Handle what?" Lydia asks when she walks in with tousled hair and wrapped in a bathrobe. She looks at us, picks up Raul's coffee cup, and takes a sip. "Needs sweetener," she gripes.

"Get your own cup," Raul snaps good-naturedly.

Lydia sticks a hand out and ruffles his hair. The two argue like brother and sister and love each other the same way. I'm glad Raul stayed here after Lydia agreed to marry me. He's been a bonus on the business end of things and Club El Diablo wouldn't be the same without him, nor would my wife.

She sticks out her tongue. "Mine won't have caffeine and it's not nice to remind me." Samson walks up to her for his morning attention. He nuzzles her stomach while Lydia scratches behind his ears.

"What are your plans today, baby?" I ask with a little more angst than I mean to. I shouldn't be jealous of the damned dog, but I really want to be the one who rubs against her belly.

Her sharp eyes miss nothing and she moves around the table and sits on my lap. "I think I'm just going to lie around and get fatter," she pouts.

"The F word so early in the morning? I'm keeping track and you won't be getting off as easily as last night."

That small spark of fire I've been waiting for enters her eyes. "There was nothing easy about getting off last night," she complains.

I arch my eyebrows at her tone.

"You need to give me a break. I'm having a fat day and I don't see it changing until this baby decides to pop out. Whining is the only way I can handle another pair of stretch pants."

I kiss her cheek and smile. Yes, I add another F word to my mental count. I know she's working to stay positive but some things just can't slide by. "Let me put a few hours in at my desk and then we can picnic at the park and take Sam with us. We'll give his dog sitter a break until this evening."

"I love you," she whispers and throws her arms around my neck.

"Just wait until tonight, though. We haven't had a serious spanking scene in weeks and I have a feeling it would help take the edge off both of us."

"I just bet you do," she adds with a soft kiss on my lips. I turn her on my lap so I can deepen the kiss. I forget Raul is even in the room, though it's nothing he hasn't seen before.

"I might puke over here."

Lydia and I turn our heads and glare. Raul grumbles while hastily leaving us to our morning kiss. He knows when to get lost and that's another reason I like him.

Chapter Twenty-Nine

Damian

A week later, because of Lydia's exhaustion, we eat a delicious dinner provided by one of the hotel chefs. Lydia enjoys cooking but she's been grumpy all day and slightly depressed. I invite Raul and his new boyfriend, Paul, to join us. Keeping my wife entertained and out of trouble these last weeks of her pregnancy is priority.

Lydia picks at her food and her mood doesn't seem to improve. I know she's not sleeping well even with that damned pillow, but there's little I can do about it. Raul suggests playing cards when the table is clear. Her mood lightens somewhat as we start a game of spades.

An hour into our quiet evening with friends, the power flickers a few times and then goes off completely and the entire penthouse goes dark.

"Lydia, do not move. I don't want you falling. The backup generators will kick in and the emergency lights will come on in a minute."

"It's a nasty storm," Paul volunteers looking toward the large rain covered floor to ceiling windows of the penthouse.

I squeeze Lydia's hand. "They've had warnings all day so this wasn't unexpected." The emergency lights come on before I finish the last of the sentence. "I need to check on the club and call the hotel's manager to make sure he has everything under control."

"I'll come with you," Lydia says.

Of course she wants to come with me. The woman has no sense of what it means to rest. "The elevators won't be working and there's no way you're walking up and down the stairway." Her hand stiffens beneath mine and her expression becomes obstinate. Before she tells me exactly how she feels about being bossed around, I lift her hand to my lips and kiss the backs of her fingers. "Argue and I'll handcuff you to the bed and give Raul the key while I'm gone."

She brings my hand to her lips and at the last minute bites me. "Once this baby is born, Master Bossy Pants, we're having a talk."

I rub my hand and the teeth marks she left behind. "As long as you begin the conversation with Master, you may be able to avoid a red ass."

"Argh, keep dreaming," she challenges.

"Don't worry, I've had months to dream up proper punishments for a disrespectful wife." I turn to Raul. "If you don't mind, I want you and Paul here with my irritating woman while I check things out."

"No problem, we'll keep her busy and out of your hair."

"Raul!" Lydia shrieks in a very un-Lydia manner.

Raul casts sheepish eyes her way. "Only while you're pregnant. I'm thinking of the baby."

"You're no friend. I'll teach Paul a few things when I'm not pregnant and you won't be sitting comfortably for a week."

"Promises, promises." Raul smiles and batts his eyelashes.

"The entire world is against me, I swear," Lydia whines again. I fight hard not to roll my eyes because I'm afraid Raul or Paul will give me away and I don't want her more agitated.

The sooner I get this done, the sooner I can put my bratty wife to bed. In her current mood she probably won't appreciate that we'll be sleeping and not playing. "I'll return as quickly as possible," I tell her before leaving.

Thirty minutes later, I've spoken to the hotel manager and assured myself that he has his end of things covered and doesn't need my help. I take a last tour of the club, which isn't crowded, thank God. Kyle and his new permanent sub, Trisha, are cuddled on a couch next to the scene area.

I check in on them before heading back to Lydia. "You hanging in there?" I ask.

Kyle nods. "We're fine. I'm assuming the elevators are out of commission until the power is back?"

"Yes and luckily we can entertain our guests for a few hours on minimal lighting if needed. The carousel isn't running but there's plenty of light to find your way around and the bar is stocked. This rarely happens, but it's not the first time we've lost power and we have a plan in place."

"We'll wait it out," Kyle assures me. He pulls Trisha closer. Her eyes are still glassy from what must have been a heavy scene. Not that Kyle plays any other way. I'm glad he's found someone who knows about his private life and accepts him for who he is. I didn't think Trisha could handle him at first, but she proved me wrong.

"Damian?" I turn and see Raul and immediately know there's a problem. "Umm, well, umm."

"What is it, Raul?" My Dom voice is filled with impatience.

"Lydia sent me to tell you her water broke."

"What?"

"She's having the baby."

Trisha pipes up from Kyle's arms. "With all the Doms around here, I'm sure someone will know what to do."

"We'll fireman-carry her down the stairs if we need to. I am not delivering a baby," I croak.

"Yes, Daddy," Trisha teases. I stare at her in horror and when I look at Raul, he has a green tint to his skin. Hell.

I ignore Trisha. "If you don't mind, will you ask if anyone in the club knows anything about childbirth? Raul, call the fire department and let them know what's happening." I take off running for the stairwell. Getting Lydia down twenty-nine flights of stairs won't be easy but she isn't having our baby outside of a hospital.

Fuck.

Chapter Thirty

Damian

I run up all four flights of stairs. We'll be carrying Lydia all the way down if the power doesn't come back on. Lydia is pacing the carpet when I enter the front room, her expression worried. I want to yell at her for walking around. We need things to slow down. Instead, I scoop her into my arms and pull her tightly against me. I press my lips to her neck and cheek.

"I love you. I promise our baby will be fine. You have my word." She immediately relaxes in my arms. I rub her back and hold her. A few minutes won't make a difference and I want her calm for the trip down the stairs. Less than a minute later, she stiffens and inhales deeply. "Breathe," I tell her because she's holding her breath and I know by the pain on her face that this is a contraction. "How long have the pains been going on, Lydia?" I ask as soon as it ends.

"A few hours," she whispers. "I'm sorry," she adds when my expression turns murderous. Now's not the time to lose my cool, so I tone it down a notch. "Why didn't you say something?"

Her lips tremble and my heart twists. She's so damn strong and independent. "I wasn't sure this was the real thing and I didn't want you worrying until I was positive."

I have so many punishments saved up for after the birth and this one will be the end all. To keep her calm, I keep my voice as gentle as I can and add a bit of teasing. "Silly momma." I kiss her nose. "Daddy needs to know these things." I lift and cradle her in my arms and for once she doesn't have a smartass comeback about her weight. "Raul should be back in a few minutes. He's calling the ambulance and Kyle is checking around the club for anyone with delivery knowledge."

Lydia's body goes taught in my arms and I decide against putting her on the couch as she battles another contraction. The damn things are close together and I have a feeling if we try to carry her down the stairs, the baby will be born in the stairwell. I head to the bedroom and wait for the pain to subside before placing her on the comforter. I grab ATG from the closet and prop it behind her back. Voices come from the other room and Trisha sticks her head inside the bedroom.

"Come in, Trish," Lydia says with a smile. I can see the strain around her mouth, but you can't hear it in her voice.

Trisha walks in with a small trail of people behind her. Kyle reaches Lydia first and kisses her cheek. "You okay, princess?"

"You're only calling me that because I can't take a whip to you right—" Pain spreads across her face. She's trembling by the time the pain ends and tears slide freely down her cheeks. She grasps my hand tightly, her nails digging into my skin. "Please, Damian, I need to talk to you alone."

That's all it takes for Kyle, Trisha, Raul, and Paul to hustle back out.

Raul whispers in my ear when he walks by, "An hour for an ambulance."

Damn. We could take the limo but I'm worried about the power outage and traffic lights. We could be caught in a jam and have the baby in the back seat. I inhale deeply and bring Lydia's hand to my lips. It's strange that I don't mind dishing out pain and pushing her limits in my dungeon, but the thought of her going through childbirth without medication is terrifying. Hell, *delivering* a child is terrifying.

Lydia buries her face against my hip when I sit on the edge of the bed. "I'm afraid," she admits. "I'm so afraid."

I press my lips to her temple. Her hand constricts on mine again and her breathing accelerates. "Slow, my love. Ride it out and breathe." I breathe along with her. She takes slow, steady breaths while her face twists in pain.

I use the side of the comforter to wipe the moisture from her brow when the pain ends. "I love you," I tell her. "I will never allow anything happen to you or our baby. In a few hours you'll be holding Abigail. I promise," I whisper. I need her to hold off giving birth until the ambulance arrives.

She gives me a small smile along with a weary sigh. "I can handle a few hours," she answers bravely.

"Of course you can. My fearless Domme can handle anything."

Her smile is brighter this time but a second later another contraction starts. It's a bad one and her small cry lets me know how bad. She's still panting when she leans in close to me. "Raul needs to hold my hand so you can deliver our daughter."

It's my turn to panic, but I can't show it. "I promised nothing would happen to you and our daughter and I mean it."

"Thank you." Her grip on my hand tightens again.

Her contractions are coming too damn fast and I know we're out of options other than delivering the baby here. My priority now is keeping her and the baby safe. "Who do you want in here with us?"

"If no one has experience delivering babies, just Raul and Trisha."

"I'll get them."

"We need towels and—" Her words cut off as another contraction hits. Lydia's loud moan fills the room.

When it's over, I rush from the room to hand out orders. Paul grabs towels and I send him to the bedroom to stay with Lydia until I'm back. Trisha fills a bowl with warm water and Raul starts boiling water on the stove.

He shrugs his shoulders when my eyebrows go up. "It's in all the movies so there must be a benefit for boiling water for childbirth."

Kyle stays out of the way, which I'm grateful for. His calm demeanor helps settle me. Once we have everything I can think of, I bring Raul and Trisha back to the room with me. Paul is holding Lydia's hand while she breathes through the latest contraction. I go to the opposite side of the bed from her and pull the comforter down. As soon as the contraction ends I pick her up.

I nod at Raul. "Place the blanket over the sheet and add a few towels."

Raul and Trisha organize the bed. Paul heads out of the room without being asked but I stop him. "Google childbirth on my tablet. It has a its own internet data connection and should still work. I need step-by-step instructions. Also check and see if there's anything else we need in here." I rest Lydia on the bed just as another contraction begins.

She grips me around the shoulders and breathes against my chest. "It hurts, Damian. I can't do this."

"Yes you can, baby. I'm here with you. We've got this." There's no longer time for terror.

"Raul, you have the honor of holding Lydia's hand. Trisha, follow me and we'll wash up." Raul and I switch places.

Trisha and I wash our hands with soap and water. She's worried too, but we're too close to Lydia and I don't want her hearing us talk, so we remain silent. Trisha is a tough woman or Kyle would never have chosen her. I don't see her buckling under with a little midwife duty.

We enter the bedroom again and Lydia is having another contraction. They appear to be on top of each other now. I take one of her nightshirts from her drawer and carry it over. "I need to remove your clothes and put you in a nightshirt."

"One of your T-shirts, please."

"Yes, my love, no problem." I toss her shirt aside and quickly grab one of mine. Hell, if she wants to wear a tutu right now, I would find her one.

Working as quickly as possible, I remove her clothes and place the soft white T-shirt over her head. She gazes up at me with trembling lips when I finish. I give her a quick, hard kiss before another contraction hits. Raul takes her hand when it ends and I move to the bottom of the bed.

"As soon as the next pain is over, we're going to move you closer to the end of the bed," I tell her like I know what I'm doing. We wait and when the pain passes, we all help guide her bottom closer to the foot of the bed, leaving room for her feet to rest on the edge of the mattress with her knees bent.

Paul enters the room again with another large bowl. He places it on the dresser and stands by the door. I walk over and speak in a low voice, "Any words of wisdom?"

Paul is a fountain of information. "Don't pull on the head, it will turn to the side naturally, and then the body will slip out. Place the baby face down on Lydia's bare tummy and cover it with a blanket or towel. Don't worry about the cord right away. If the paramedics aren't here shortly, we'll go to the next step."

"Thanks, I need to have a look and see what's going on. Any advice there?"

"If you can see the baby's head, it's time. Have her push with the pain."

Lydia starts groaning again and Paul steps from the room. I go back to work. "When this pain is over, I'm going to have a look," I tell her with a confidence I don't feel.

"Shut the fuck up and just let me deal with this pain," she yells.

Her attitude makes me smile and I take a deep breath. "Yes, dear," I reply as sweetly as possible. Scared Lydia isn't easy to handle, but now the real Lydia is back. Having a baby outside the hospital is definitely something she can handle.

"Fuck you," she snaps back at me.

"I knew your potty mouth would activate sooner or later," I mumble.

The pain ends and I move her legs wider apart to check on the baby's progress. The head isn't showing yet. I rest my hand on her thigh and begin rubbing the skin to soothe her.

"Don't touch my legs," she cries.

It's like touching a hot surface and I jerk my hand away. "Yes, ma'am," I say while fighting laughter. She's so damn bossy and there's no reason childbirth would be different.

"I swear if you're laughing at me, we're getting divorced." Another pain takes over.

I change places with Trisha, who is on the opposite side of Raul. I take Lydia's hand expecting to be snapped at again. She releases Raul and rolls slightly toward me. She grasps my hand and groans through the pain.

"I don't think I can do this," she says when it subsides.

"You're wrong," I tell her with confidence. "I have no doubt you can do this."

"But I had it all arranged," she cries. "They were giving me an epidural as soon as I got to the hospital. My doctor promised."

I kiss her cheek and smooth hair from the side of her face. "I love you. You will be a wonderful mother and we're almost ready to welcome our daughter."

Her breathing picks up along with the pressure on my hand. I sit with her wishing I could take the pain away. The contractions grow steadily and then seem to slow. I check with Paul and he tells me that's normal when it's getting close. Raul and Trisha both look as terrified as I feel. I do everything I can to show them and Lydia that we can do this.

I'll check her again in ten minutes. She's moaning nonstop now and I'm completely helpless to take the pain away.

"Red, red, oh, God," she screams.

My heart clenches. "Your Domme is the baby right now and she's stubborn like mommy and not listening."

"Mommy always listens to red. I can't take this. Please help me." Now my heart breaks.

I look up at Raul. He walks around to my side of the bed and takes my place. Trisha moves to the other side and I check to see if Lydia's made progress.

There's a small amount of blood on the towel beneath her. I move her knees apart and see a tuft of dark hair. *Thank God*, I think to myself. "It's time, baby," I whisper.

"No shit, Sherlock. She's killing me and I need to push," she groans.

I turn to Raul and he's fighting laughter like me. Trisha gives us both a stern look, but I see the merriment in her eyes.

Another pain begins and I can see more of my daughter's hair. It's not really dark. No, it's short and red. *Oh Abby, you will give your father a merry chase.*

"She's almost here, Lydia, push with the pain and then stop when I tell you to."

"I will do no su…ahhh, it hurts."

"Raul, get on the bed behind her and help her sit a little."

Raul moves fast and situates himself so he can hold Lydia.

"Trisha, prepare a blanket and hand it to me when I ask." I'm using my authoritative voice for Lydia's benefit. I know it will keep her calm. I also hide my shaking hands because that will do the opposite.

The pain slows and more coaching begins when the next one starts. "You need to push, Lydia, push hard."

"I can't. Please, I can't."

"I'm going to slap your ass for that one. Push damn it!"

Her face tightens and she pushes. The baby's head is almost out.

"Hold on, Lydia, no pushing right now. Wait for the pain."

"I'm going to kill you. It's your fault the power went out and you got me into this mess with your wiggly squiggles. I'm better off swallowing," she wails.

If I look at anyone, I won't be able to control my laughter. Trisha makes a slight noise but manages to keep herself together. When the next pain starts, Lydia screams with a final push and our daughter enters the world. I stand looking at my bloody hands holding the most precious gift in the universe and feel tears well in my eyes. Her small slippery frame is perfect. Her eyes are open and her tiny face scrunched up as she lets loose with a solid cry, which grows louder with each passing second.

I look into Lydia's sweat-covered face. "I love you." I place a kiss on Abby's head and lift her to Lydia's exposed belly. Trisha hands me the blanket she's holding, and I cover Lydia and the baby.

Paul walks in. "I'll go check on the ambulance."

I slide onto the bed beside my wife and don't take my eyes from her and the baby. Everyone files out and the door closes behind them. I kiss Lydia's hair and inhale her scent. "You're my world, baby. Thank you for my daughter."

Her hand smooths over the crown of the baby's head. "She's beautiful."

I'm looking at Lydia when I answer. "Breathtaking. I want another next year."

She laughs and says, "Not going to happen." She smiles at me with so much love. I'm finally able to breathe.

Holly S. Roberts

Chapter Thirty-One

Damian

Five minutes after Abigail is born, the electricity comes on. Five minutes after that, paramedics take over. I grab Lydia's pre-packed travel bag and follow them to the ambulance.

Doctor Pastavich, Lydia's OB/GYN is waiting at the hospital. All our preplanning is out the window, but I'm able to cut the cord. A nurse takes Abigail away so they can check her out thoroughly. Lydia requires stitches and I hold her hand while the doctor works.

A short time later, tightly bundled in a pink blanket, the nurse places Abigail back into Lydia's arms. She's sucking dramatically on her fist and we all smile.

"She's doing wonderfully considering how she made her appearance. A pediatrician looked her over. He'll be in to see you soon. Right now this little one needs to eat." The nurse helps Lydia with her hospital gown.

Lydia lifts the baby to her breast and pinches her nipple, rubbing it against the small pert mouth. Abigail's head makes a searching movement before she finds what she's looking for and latches on.

In my entire life, I've never seen anything more amazing. And fucking sexy. I laugh at myself acknowledging what a kinky bastard I am. I fit my finger into Abigail's tiny hand and she squeezes. I can't stop myself from leaning over and gently pressing my lips to Lydia's.

"I love you so much and I'm so damn proud of you. Our daughter is beautiful and looks just like her mommy. I wanted red hair and got all my wishes in one small bundle."

Lydia smiles lovingly back. "I can't believe she only weighs six pounds. I thought she would weigh at least fifteen with all the weight I gained."

I lean closer so we're nose to nose. "If you use the F word I'll gag you right here at the hospital. You're beautiful and every pound gives me more to love. I'll miss each one you lose and rejoice in every pound I can convince you to keep."

"Yes, Sir."

I lean back and slide my finger across the breast my daughter is feeding from. "I'm quite jealous of our daughter, you know?"

Lydia's eyes sparkle with mirth because she knows what a kinky bastard I am too. "It will be a few days before my milk comes in, but as soon as it does, I promise you a taste."

"It's going to be impossible to keep my hands off you for the next six weeks."

"Well good. I have no intention of keeping my hands off you and I'll enjoy driving you crazy for a change."

"I guarantee you'll be securing my hands for that to work."

She grins and I know we're both thinking about the last time she bound my hands to the headboard and I broke it. My sweet Domme was quite unhappy.

"We still need a nanny," she says with a yawn.

My soft groan makes her grin widen. We've gone around and around with this one. Our kinky lifestyle makes it difficult to find someone who won't run screaming the first time she sees us in club garb. I wish my mother lived closer. Without her we'll be taking turns working at the club. "We'll start looking again next week." I touch Lydia's nose with the end of my finger. "I thought money bought everything," I grumble.

Her laughter fills the room. "We'll find someone. I'm sure your money will buy a great nanny." Another yawn follows this statement and she closes her eyes. I rest my hand on the baby's back and watch my family sleep.

     ***

It's late afternoon of the second day before we're cleared to return home. After the nurses poked and prodded Lydia and the baby for two days, we're ready for uninterrupted family time. The hospital staff was terrific and we knew they were only doing their jobs. Abigail is doing wonderfully and home is where we need to be.

Raul and Paul prepare for our arrival and have the bassinet and baby monitor set up in the master bedroom. They leave pre-made meals in the refrigerator and if we run out, the hotel staff is at our beck and call. It will be so nice to relax with absolutely nothing on our agenda but taking care of our new addition.

We spoke at length about Samson and the baby before we introduced them. We needn't have worried. It was instant love on Sam's part and he whines non-stop whenever Abigail is out of sight. We discover there's no need for the baby monitor because Sam's ears pick up the slightest noise. If we don't go to Abigail immediately, his low whine turns to a full-on howling bark. It's also fun to watch him when others are around the baby. We have no doubt blood will spill if anyone harms her.

My mother stays with us the first week after we return from the hospital. Lydia is fully aware of our side business and she came along with me twice before she got pregnant. Between morning sickness and her growing belly, she stopped coming until after the birth. She and my mother talk about the women they're helping. Lydia is now fully involved in plans for their care. I set up a bank account so she can provide whatever my mother and the women need. Watching my mother with Abby is priceless and our small family couldn't be more perfect.

Mom and Lydia cry their eyes out when it's time to say goodbye. We agree to a trip to her place in a few months so the women can meet Abigail. A few days later, we have a small gathering in the penthouse and move Samson to Raul's suite so there are no mishaps with too many people holding Abigail. Bran and Willow are back from their honeymoon and they join us, along with other regulars from the club. It's nice to have friends around, but Lydia is exhausted by the time everyone leaves. I tuck my wife and baby into their respective beds and Lydia is out cold before I leave the room. Abigail will sleep for at least two hours and I need to check on the club.

Raul and Paul are doing a great job. There haven't been any problems that required my attention and for that alone I'm grateful. I walk past a station and see Bran working a scene with my sister. Definitely not something I'm comfortable watching, so I move on. Yeah, Bran thought he could leave the lifestyle. How wrong he was and even though I have no intention of watching him scene with my sister, I'm glad they have each other.

After I'm assured things are running smoothly, I head back to the penthouse. After checking on Abigail in the bassinet by the bed, I crawl in beside his wife, pulling her close and kiss the back of her head. She never stirs. I exhale in contentment and fall asleep.

Chapter Thirty-Two

Damian

It's been four weeks since Abigail was born and our life now revolves around a recently weighed in seven pound ten ounce bundle of fluff. Her feeding schedule gives us about two and a half contented hours and then she turns into a devil child.

Her eyes are going from blue to green like Lydia's and her hair is growing curlier, thicker, and a more defined red. She follows her admirers with her eyes and graces them with quick smiles and contented gurgles when we least expect it. How our lives have changed.

I have the pleasure of spending the next hour alone with her highness while Lydia goes to the gym to work out for the first time since Abby's birth.

"Do not overdo it and that's an order," I tell her with the sternest expression I can muster.

"Yes, Daddy."

I give my customary growl because she knows she's pushing my buttons by calling me Daddy after I give her an order. Abigail's head rests on my shoulder so I can burp her since Lydia fed her right before she left. Samson walks beside me as I cross the room and turn back to repeat my carpet march.

After her highness gives an unladylike burp, we sit on the couch and I lightly bounce Abby up and down on my lap. Samson stays on guard and keeps a close eye on his baby much like a mother lion. We're both good with our parental duties until a gallon of curdled milk spews from Abigail's dainty mouth.

"Oh damn," I whisper and look around. Samson the traitor takes a few steps back. There's nothing in the immediate vicinity to wipe off the aftereffects of a baby volcano. "Damn," I say again a little louder. It's either my tone or volume that sets Abigail off. A few whimpers turn to screams within thirty seconds. Of course Samson doesn't help and his short whines go into full on howls to rival Abby's screams.

I stare at the dog with my best Dom eyes. "Really, you think you're helping?" Samson steps forward and sniffs the curdled milk. Before I can stop him, he slurps up a large section of chunky breast milk and I gag. My first experience alone with my daughter is quickly going from bad to worse. I jump up and head to the bathroom while Abigail continues screaming. Samson's howls grow longer and louder if that's even possible. "Why me?" I mutter.

Cleaning the baby up with a wet washcloth only makes her angrier. I lay her on the bed with her little arms and legs flapping in an angry tirade so I can change my shirt. She doesn't like that, so I think better of it. Thank God Lydia can't see what a disaster I've made of daddy daycare. I pick up Abby and pace for ten minutes before I finally give in and reach for my cell.

"I'll be right up," Raul says without me saying a word. The commotion in the background must have been enough to let him know I'm in desperate straits. My wife is gone for twenty minutes and her big bad Dom is reduced to calling big bad gay backup.

Raul doesn't bother knocking and enters using the penthouse key code. He takes Abby from my arms mid—I swear she isn't breathing—scream. He ignores her wails and changes her clothes and diaper with me watching over his shoulder. Lifting her to his chest, he rubs her back to soothe her. He flashes Samson a chilling look and says, "No," in a soft voice that the damn dog actually listens to. One instant Abigail and the dog are in tandem and the next the room is completely silent.

I run my hand over my head. "I can't believe you just did that."

Raul smiles slightly and nuzzles Abigail's chubby neck. "It's a gay uncle thing."

"And Samson?"

He reaches down and pets Sam's head. "I've known this dog since he was Abby's age. He just needs to know his baby is safe."

"And her daddy doesn't keep her safe?" I question.

Raul's grin is getting on my nerves. "Not in dog language."

"Christ! He licked up her vomit and I almost lost my lunch." Raul doesn't even try to contain his laughter. "What's it going to cost me to keep this quiet?"

Raul laughs harder. "I'll think of something and collect another time. Do you want me to put her in the bassinet? I think she's sleeping now."

Abby's little eyes are closed and she's once again a content princess. "Yeah, put her down and I'll let Sam outside. Maybe he'll regurgitate baby puke on the grass and I'll have another picture that needs to be exorcised from my brain."

"After that, please change your shirt. You smell a little spoiled."

Chapter Thirty-Three

Damian

Our nanny interviews are unsuccessful over the next two weeks. I'm back at the club most evenings and Lydia is growing grouchier each day.

It's the busy season with out of town travelers arriving in droves. I perform two basic scenes with experienced subs who don't need sexual stimulation. I'm ready to have my wife back and she's all I can think about. Lydia has no problem giving me blow jobs but we're both at the point where kinky sex is what we really need. Aftercare with the second sub is tricky because my cock swells with thoughts of my wife when I should be thinking about the woman I'm holding.

It takes three minutes to decide that this isn't working, so I fetch Celia a drink of water and hand over orange slices before letting her go to the bar to visit with friends. There's no way I'm doing another scene tonight. I notice a crowd gathering at one of the stations and decide to check it out before calling it a night.

"Damn," I mutter under my breath when I see who has everyone's attention.

It's Lydia—fuller, sexier, and more luscious than ever. My cock goes rock hard before I inhale another breath. Her thick red hair hangs down her almost bare back in glorious waves. She's wearing a black leather bra that barely contains her large nursing breasts. The black leather short skirt only covers the top of her ass and I'm not sure if she's wearing a thong or nothing at all beneath it. Damn. Her high heel boots end just below her knees. A softly rounded post-baby belly pokes out slightly and adds to the hot scene in front of me.

Lydia winks at me before giving her full attention to a male sub strapped face first to the St. Andrew's Cross. Gripping his hair, she pulls his head back and kisses him with aggressive passion. My cock doubles in size. She takes his bottom lip between her teeth and pulls slightly and I actually groan. She releases the sub's lip and runs her tongue up the side of his jaw. Yeah that one almost makes me come in my tight leather pants.

She's playing with me and she knows I'm putty in her hands. I stay in the background and enjoy the scene. Lydia takes a metal anal ball and cock ring from the tray beside her. She places her hand on her lucky sub's thigh and puts the ring around his balls. Next she inserts the ball into his ass while he squirms. *Lucky bastard*, I think to myself. His movement earns him a not-so-tender slap on his upper thigh very close to the cock ring.

Lydia backs up and admires her handiwork. She grabs one of her favorite torture devices and unfurls the three feet of leather. Fuck, just the image of her holding that whip is enough to cause an extra ache in my balls. *Hell, becoming a sub is looking better and better.* Yeah that last thought proves it's been entirely too long since I've been with my wife.

She rolls her shoulders before releasing the whip with a resounding snap. Her anxious sub jumps even though the whip lands nowhere near him. She glances around at her audience and stops on me. The look in her eyes is hot as hell. I nod and she turns back to her sub.

I love the way she uses the whip as an extension of her arm. Within a few minutes, faint red stripes appear across his back, ass, and upper thighs. She's catching him with just the popper, which doesn't actually hurt. He twists and moans because the fucker is turned on.

Her precision is impeccable and I realize she's probably practicing during her forays to the gym. The club is quiet at that time of day and I would bet she's using one of the private rooms. My wife has mad skills with a whip. She also has a way of entertaining an audience. They stand in thrall of her scene. God, I've missed this.

The whip portion of the scene is over as quickly as it began. Lydia lays the whip down before removing the anal plug and cock ring. She unfastens her sub from his bindings. Poor guy never had an orgasm. My wife knows exactly how to leave someone hanging.

It occurs to me that Raul, who usually helps Lydia with scenes, must be babysitting. If that's the case, I owe Raul another favor.

Lydia takes her sub's hand and leads him to a couch for aftercare. I receive another wink when she passes. Oh, she'll pay for that one. I move with her and stand at the side of the large planter watching my wife speak quietly to her sub. She knows I'm here and she takes advantage by rubbing oil over his body while they talk. The people here love her. She has a way of making them feel special even when her husband is standing a few feet away.

Finally, she wipes her hands on a towel and helps him stand. She adds a gentle kiss to his cheek. "Schedule with me next week, Caleb, and we'll work on a few things to help you. The front office will set you up."

"Thank you, Mistress Lydia," he replies with obvious hero worship.

She smiles and squeezes his arm. "Enjoy yourself the rest of the evening."

"Thank you, Mistress." He walks away with a smile.

I wait impatiently as Lydia gathers her whip and a few other props. I'm a foot away when she turns. I pull her hard against my chest. "Put those four inch heels around my back," I whisper in her ear as I lift her. "We're going to our own private playroom."

"Yes, Daddy." Desire oozes. She locks her legs around me and I carry her straight to my office. No one is dumb enough to stop us and we take the private elevator without interruption.

"Who's with Abigail?" I ask as an afterthought.

"Our new nanny."

That surprises me because we've found no one we can both agree on. "Do I have any say over the new nanny?" I keep my voice even, wishing I hadn't asked. This is no time to argue with my delectable wife.

"Her name is Raul and she turned in her application today. She has every qualification we want. She's giving notice at her current job tomorrow."

"Hell, why didn't he apply months ago?"

She offers a tight smile. "He didn't think we would want a gay man helping to raise our daughter."

The elevator doors open. "That's the dumbest thing I've ever heard. He's perfect and quite frankly more natural at it than me," I grumble.

Her smile turns mischievous. She leans in and bites my earlobe before adding, "Don't worry, Mommy has better uses for Daddy, and he'll be really good at what she has planned."

"Mommy's done enough planning for a while. Her Dom is making his demands for the next year or so and she'll need to wait."

"Yum, that sounds like kinky fun."

I don't reply, I just carry her to our private dungeon.

We both feel the wetness on the front of us at the same time. "Oops. Maybe I should pump first."

"Over my dead body. Seeing you run your hands over that sub's body is more than I can handle after leaving you alone for six weeks. I'm not waiting."

Her eyes snap fire. "I told you two weeks ago that I could play."

I lean away slightly so she sees my glare. "I have a special ball gag for feisty subs." She presses her lips together and doesn't answer. Smart little sub. As hard as it was to wait, I wanted to be sure she was ready. I watched the doctor stitch her after Abigail's birth and I wanted to be damn sure she healed.

The wait is paying off tonight.

Chapter Thirty-Four

Damian

I sit her ass on a high bench and go to my knees to remove her boots. I take my time and massage the instep of each foot because I know this is her first time back in heels. She makes small sounds, which are nothing compared to the ones she'll be singing later. I rise and pull her forward so she's standing in front of me. I unzip her skirt and slowly peel the material over her hips. Naughty, naughty girl. She's completely bare from waist down. I turn her around and unclip her bra, sliding the straps over her arms until it falls to the floor. Taking her hand, I lead her to the cross and secure her so she's facing me. With a wicked smile, I place a blindfold over her eyes.

I leave her in all her beautiful glory and turn on soft sultry music to set the scene. I want her thinking about what's coming next while I fetch a few things from our room. The waiting will drive her crazy, which is half the fun. I glance into Abigail's bassinet but she's not there. I check in the nursery and Raul is holding a quiet Abby. Samson is on guard duty next to the rocking chair where Raul is gently gliding back and forth.

"She had a bottle of breast milk and I'll put her down in a minute," Raul whispers.

"Thank you. You and I will have a talk soon about your delay in taking up the nanny position. I'm glad you finally tapped into that brain in your head."

"Yes, Sir." Raul smiles.

I answer him with a smile of my own. "There's a very dirty job I must attend to in the dungeon and this might take most of the night."

His thumb comes up in encouragement. "Enjoy yourself."

My sweet sub turns her head when I walk back into the dungeon. I don't say anything because the silence drives her crazy. She really hates ball gags and we'll see if she survives the night without one.

I move closer and admire her engorged breasts. They must be painful. I slowly trace one finger along the blue vein just under the skin of one hard globe.

"Ahhh, they hurt," she complains.

I pinch her nipple just a bit and the opaque liquid instantly covers my fingertips. "I know and I plan to make them hurt more," I promise.

I lean in and suck gently, drinking her sweet milk. When it flows freely, I place the breast pump around her nipple, turn the machine on, and suction the milk into the attached bottle. Her other breast drips during the entire process.

Only a few years ago I wouldn't have understood my current fascination with breast milk and the eroticism of a nursing wife. Now, I hope Lydia breastfeeds for as long as possible. When the first breast isn't quite as hard, I suck gently on the other to prepare it. She squirms and makes sweet noises of relief as the pressure fades. When both breasts are properly milked, I cap the bottle and date the label. There's a small refrigerator in the corner with an equally small freezer for me to place the milk. I take my time rinsing the pump so it's ready for its next use.

Lydia's foot tapping doesn't escape me, but this is her punishment for making me watch her with tonight's sub after weeks of celibacy. Just thinking about it makes my cock rage again. It's time to play with my naughty wife.

I move up next to her and whisper in her ear, "I'm surprised you've managed to stay quiet."

"Will it do me any good to scream?" Her voice is silky smooth.

I skim my fingers across the flesh of her upper breasts and watch her nipple tighten. "No, but I love when your mouth is filled with a gag or my cock."

"I'm being good, Daddy," she says with obvious manipulation. Lydia is always a bratty sub and we both know it.

"You are, for now. I find myself unable to forget the play scene you performed earlier tonight. I've been saving so many punishments and you did yourself no favors by pulling that stunt."

It's her turn to give me a wicked smile. "I wanted you worked up and your cock hard."

I hold back a groan. "My cock has been hard for six weeks." I remove my hand and move away from her. I grin and pretend not to hear her moan of displeasure.

The next time I approach her, I remove my shoes first so she doesn't hear me. She jumps when I place the cold metal of a nipple clamp against her skin. "These are tweezer clamps and shouldn't be too uncomfortable or cause problems with your milk production." I studied the subject in preparation for our return to kinky play.

"Daddy did his homework," she says. A low moan follows as I attach the first clamp and then the other.

Next, I grab my favorite toy. It's a vibrating butt plug and it always leaves her a squirting mess. I liberally lube the plug and my fingers. I place my hand between the cross and her ass cheeks to tip her farther out so I can play with her ass a little before sliding the plug in. Her hips jerk at the contact.

"It's probably uncomfortable because you've had no action back here for a while," I tell her just to piss her off.

My statement does the trick. "It's hurts because Daddy isn't playing anywhere else."

"Hmm," I contemplate. "I'll take that under advisement."

I slide another finger inside and she wiggles as her body becomes accustomed to the stretch. When I know she's ready, I replace my fingers with the plug, which is much bigger than she likes.

"Ahh, you bastard," she moans when it's finally seated properly.

"You're one word away from the gag," I warn.

Her teeth clamp shut. I leave her alone once the plug is in place and wash my hands before choosing another toy. "These clamps have a little more bite but I want your pussy open for the flogger."

Back in the early days of taking over my father's sex toy company, I designed these babies. They consist of two soft straps of leather with Velcro. Each has a clamp attached, which I use to spread her red, swollen pussy lips.

I pick up one of the soft floggers. I can be gentle with it or cause a bit of sting if she misbehaves. The first strike hits her belly and she squeals.

"Does my sweet little sub like that?"

"Yes." Her breath huffs out when I strike the side of her hip.

The displayed folds of her pussy are waiting, but they will continue to wait. I switch targets between her stomach, hips, and thighs. Occasionally I softly strike her breasts knowing the nipple clamps add to the sensation. It takes fifteen minutes before she starts begging.

"Please, oh God, please I need to come."

It's exactly what I've been waiting for. I click the switch on the remote in my pocket and the butt plug vibrates.

Her hips thrust forward. "Arghhh, please, ahhhh."

The next two strikes of the flogger land on her dripping pussy and I switch off the vibrator.

Between gasps for air, my sweet wife shows her true colors. "Fuck you, I'm punished already, please just fuck me. I'll suck you off if you want, but please FUCK me. Now!"

I turn the anal plug back on and cross my arms to watch her buck against the restraints. I switch off the plug when she's about to lose her shit. Her scream of frustration is long and loud. I move directly in front of her and go to my knees. Her pussy is so damn swollen. I re-adjust the pussy clamps from back to front and hit the switch on the plug as soon as they're where I want them.

She grinds her hips, unable to find relief. She stays quiet, though, and I know she's going inside her head to concentrate on having an orgasm whether I want her to or not. I turn off the plug and remove the clamps from her nipples, which hurts like a bitch when all the blood rushes back to them. When she stops moaning, I unstrap her legs and then her arms until she slumps against me.

"I'm carrying you to the spanking bench. No wiggling." Her heavy breathing is my only answer. I arrange her on her stomach on the bench with her legs spread and the clamps pulling on her drenched pussy.

I place a steadying hand on her lower back. "I'm doing the counting because each transgression you've committed over the past few months is stored in my brain. I'll know when I'm done."

Her voice trembles and tears slide down her cheeks. "Are you going to fuck me when you're finished with my punishment?"

My balls tighten at her desperation. "I'm thinking about it."

"You had better think hard."

My palm lands with a sharp *thwap* at her disrespectful tone. And it begins. I mentally count every transgression. Her potty mouth gains her ten; stubbornness, refusal to follow my orders in the bedroom, driving me crazy every chance she gets, and last but not least tonight's misadventures account for the rest. Every cry helps me regain that Dom head space I've been missing. She's begging when I count the last ten out loud. She hasn't used her safe word and I'm proud of her.

"We're almost done, sweetness, but I just remembered something." I turn on the butt plug and give her the final five. "I don't know about you but I feel better," I say when I'm done. Yeah that's a lie. My cock is one swollen nerve set to explode at the slightest touch.

"Fuck you," she gasps like the Lydia I know so well.

"Oh, I think you will." I quickly remove my clothes and last but not least, I take out the butt plug. In one steady thrust I bury my cock in her ass until I'm balls deep.

"You feel so fucking good," I groan against her back.

"Please just give me a minute. Please," she begs desperately.

"Oh, sweetness. Your punishment's over, so I can afford to be nice." I trail kisses across the center of her back to gain control of myself. I grab the clamps on her pussy and pull them off. Blood quickly rushes into the lips of her pussy and she arches against me.

"That wasn't nice," she hisses.

"But this is." I pull out and push back inside the tight channel that's squeezing my cock. She's so damn snug and the pressure in my balls increases. I work myself in and out finding a steady pace that leaves us both gasping for air.

"Please, Master, may I come?" She's shuddering beneath me.

"Yes, come for me, sweet Lydia." The heavy contraction in her ass makes me increase my thrusts but she's past caring. I can no longer hold back and my cock explodes with pent-up need. Our moans and animalistic sounds fill the room. So damn good. This woman is everything I've ever needed. I collapse against her back and hold her as tightly as I can without hurting her.

Eventually, we head to the shower and I gently wash her from head to toe. "Do you need to pump?" I ask when I feel her breasts are hard again.

She smiles softly, totally replete in sub zone. "I would prefer your kinky lips do the work."

Between nipping kisses, I tell her exactly what I think about my current job. "My kinky mouth will always be at your disposal. I love you and I'm so glad you're ready for me because Daddy's hungry."

Her sighs of pleasure fill the shower.

A note from Holly

Rewriting the original novella and giving Damian and Lydia a longer story was a lot of fun. It was so nice to revisit the Club and get back into my kink groove. I also love the new Club covers that my graphic designer came up with. Subtle yet enticing via the very talented Fantasia Frog Designs.

I have so many people to thank and I'll begin with my editor Michelle Kowalski. I've lost count of the number of books we've worked on together. She takes this dyslexic woman's ideas and makes me appear grammar intelligent. I've learned so much from her and wouldn't be half the writer I am today without her help. My street team pulls the weight when I'm in my writing cave. You ladies rock Facebook and I love you for it. My husband keeps me sane, fed, and bathed during the stress of deadlines. He also gives me plenty of kinky ideas. We'll say he's multi-talented.

My readers are the best. Thank you for all your support. I'm still amazed that people read my work and I love you for it.

If you enjoyed Damian and Lydia's story, there's more from Club El Diablo:

Zachery & Monroe
Monroe & Zachery

Krispen
Stephon & Matt
Luke

For a complete list of my books visit *wickedstorytelling.com*

Love and Kisses,
Holly

www.ingramcontent.com/pod-product-compliance
Lightning Source LLC
Chambersburg PA
CBHW022008170626
46808CB00001B/319